Promises,
Promises

clearwater crossing

Promises, Promises

laura peyton roberts

BANTAM BOOKS
NEW YORK • TORONTO • LONDON • SYDNEY • AUCKLAND

RL 5.8, age 12 and up
PROMISES, PROMISES
A Bantam Book / August 1998

All scripture quotations, unless otherwise indicated, are taken from
the HOLY BIBLE, NEW INTERNATIONAL VERSION®. NIV®.
Copyright © 1973, 1978, 1984 by International Bible Society. Used by
permission of Zondervan Publishing House. All rights reserved.

ISBN 0-553-57127-3

Published simultaneously in the United States and Canada.

Bantam Books are published by Bantam Books, a division of Bantam
Doubleday Dell Publishing Group, Inc. Its trademark, consisting of the
words "Bantam Books" and the portrayal of a rooster, is Registered in
U.S. Patent and Trademark Office and in other countries. Marca Reg-
istrada. Bantam Books, 1540 Broadway, New York, New York 10036.

PRINTED IN THE UNITED STATES OF AMERICA

CWO   10 9 8 7 6 5 4 3 2 1

For Megan

It is better not to vow than to make a vow and not fulfill it.

Ecclesiastes 5:5

One

"A re you almost done in there or what?" Miguel del Rios called to his younger sister, Rosa, through the closed bathroom door. "We're going to be late for school."

"It's my turn, Miguel," she replied testily. "You already had a turn."

"Yeah, but that was *before* breakfast. Now I have to brush my teeth and then we have to go."

The door opened abruptly. Fifteen-year-old Rosa filled the doorway, her shoulder-length black hair freshly styled into a smooth, slightly curved ponytail. She wore no makeup, but the contrast of her dark eyes and brows against her light olive skin was pronounced, and a constant, natural flush gave her the appearance of blushing anyway. Her lips gleamed under a coat of clear gloss.

"I'm ready," she announced, flicking some imaginary lint from the front of her immaculate plaid school jumper. "Happy?"

"Yeah, yeah," he muttered, wriggling by her in the limited space. He grabbed his toothbrush out of the holder, laid down a thick rope of tooth-paste, and began running it hurriedly around in his mouth.

The fact that it was Tuesday didn't matter. Every morning was the exact same thing: he and Rosa jockeying for position in the bathroom while their mom made them breakfast and, if they wanted them, sack lunches. *It's a good thing Mom doesn't need to get in here until after we leave, or then we would have a problem*, he thought, spitting a wad of white foam down the drain. He wondered if a similar scene was in progress at the Rosenthal con-dominium. It didn't seem likely—it was nearly im-possible to imagine Leah ever being as late or disorganized as he and Rosa always were.

Leah. Just the thought of her name curved his mouth into a smile. He could still barely believe she'd won the Missouri portion of a national modeling contest for the U.S. Girls clothing chain. Not that he was surprised the judges had picked her—he just couldn't believe she'd entered. *Nicole must have really begged*, he laughed to himself, loving the idea that Leah had gone onstage to support a friend and had accidentally ended up winning.

"I thought you were in a hurry," Rosa said point-edly from the hallway behind him; he hadn't closed the door. Her book bag was over her shoulder now, and she held out his sack lunch at arm's length. "Shall we go?"

"I'm just waiting for you," he told her, grabbing the bag.

Rosa rolled her brown eyes and walked away into the living room, Miguel right behind her. Mrs. del Rios was lying on the sofa in her favorite old bathrobe.

"Mom, what's the matter?" Miguel asked anxiously, feeling his stomach tighten down on his breakfast. "Are you okay?"

"I'm fine," his mother said hurriedly. She struggled into a sitting position. "Don't worry about me, *mi hijo*."

"Do you want me to take you to the doctor?" Miguel asked, not in the least reassured. He knelt in front of the sofa and squeezed his mother's thin hands. "I can miss school today, Mom. I'll make it up—it's no big deal."

"It's a big deal to me. Besides, I'm fine. I'm just a little tired this morning, is all."

"Do you promise?"

"Of course, *mi amor*." She leaned forward and kissed his cheek. "Please, if you want to help me, get the two of you to school on time. You should have left ten minutes ago."

"You ought to stay home from work today," Rosa told her mother. "Don't walk over there if you're already tired. Let someone else answer the phones."

3

Before she'd become ill, Mrs. del Rios had held a sales position in the women's clothing section of a local department store. But now those hours were too long and inflexible, the standing too exhausting. These days she worked part-time in the office of All Souls Roman Catholic Church.

"She's right," Miguel interjected quickly. "Call them up and tell them you're not coming."

"I will if I don't feel better soon. Now go." She kissed him again and stood to kiss Rosa as well. "Have a good day at school."

"Like it's possible to have a good day anymore," Miguel grumbled when he and Rosa were safely inside the car, out of his mother's hearing. "Why don't they just do the transplant already?"

Rosa cast him an impatient look. "Because they don't have a donor kidney, obviously. We have to wait our turn."

"I'm sick and tired of waiting!" He started the car and began driving in the direction of Sacred Heart Academy, the all-girls Catholic school Rosa attended on scholarship. Miguel still didn't understand why his sister had chosen Sacred Heart over Clearwater Crossing High School, but that was where she'd wanted to go. "Besides," he added, "we've already waited. We've been waiting for almost two years! And where has it gotten us? Still on dialysis three times a week, that's where. Mom ought to just let me give her one of my kidneys. We can't go on like this forever."

Rosa twisted around in the passenger seat. "It's not going to be forever, Miguel. I'm worried about Mom the same as you, but she's right not to take your kidney. If you got kidney disease too or were in an accident and lost the other one, you'd be much worse off than she is now. Because you're *young*, Miguel. A lot could happen."

"But I ought to be doing something!"

Rosa shook her head. "You know there's nothing you can do. We just have to be patient and trust God to take care of us."

"Oh, right," Miguel sneered, his voice dripping bitterness. "Like he took care of Dad! Thanks anyway, Rosa, but I wasn't too happy with the way that turned out."

Rosa turned quickly away, and Miguel half regretted his angry words. Watching their father die of cancer hadn't been easy for Rosa, either. But Miguel wouldn't take back what he'd said. Any god who'd put good people through something like that wasn't one he was interested in believing in anymore, let alone in trusting patiently. No, there had to be another way.

It was so frustrating that no one would let him donate the kidney his mother needed. If everyone weren't so wrapped up in the fact that he was only seventeen, they'd have to admit that that was the best option. His mother had the kind of long-term kidney disease that resulted in kidney failure. Hemodialysis—a process that used a machine instead of kidneys to clean the toxins from her blood—was the only thing keeping her alive. But not only did dialysis take about three hours per appointment, there were side effects of the disease and treatment that over time had contributed to his mother's generally poor state of health.

The only good way the ordeal could end was for Mrs. del Rios to get a new kidney from a donor. She didn't need two; one was enough. But there were thousands of people in the same predicament—and on the waiting list—and there was no telling when it would finally be Miguel's mother's turn. Not only that, but donor kidneys didn't always survive the transplant. Sometimes they were rejected by their new bodies, despite the antirejection drugs recipients took for the rest of their lives. The best way, the *fastest* way, was to get a kidney from a family member. Someone related by blood. Someone like Miguel.

He sighed impatiently as he turned the final corner before Rosa's school. He *knew* how to make his mother well. The problem was no one would let him. For the hundredth time, he considered talking the situation over with Leah. Leah would understand how he felt. She might even have some good ideas.

A moment later he shook his head. *You should*

have done that up front, when you told her about your father, he thought. *She's going to be good and mad if she finds out you've been keeping something so important a secret all this time.*

He wished now that he *had* told her. It just hadn't seemed pertinent at the time. Later, when he knew he should say something, it had seemed strange to bring it up out of the blue, especially when he hadn't mentioned it before. Of course, the more time went by, the more strange mentioning it at all began to seem. He just wasn't a talker—that was the problem. Whatever the impulse was that made people want to spill their deepest secrets, he was positive he'd never felt it. He *hated* to talk about personal things, in fact. He hated it more than practically anything.

Because Miguel believed in the power of words. Deep in his heart he suspected that simply saying his father was dead or his mother was ill was enough to make those things true. It was almost as if nothing truly existed, or at least was truly permanent, until it was spoken out loud. And then it was over. Then it was etched in stone.

He couldn't tell Leah his mother had end-stage kidney disease. Because then he'd have to believe it himself.

Jesse Jones turned his BMW down the private road to the Andrewses' house and spotted Melanie already on her way to the corner. She was walking along the edge of the pavement in a short red coat over a navy miniskirt. Thick thigh-high socks protected her legs from the cold, and her butterscotch-blond hair streamed out behind her, shinier than ever in the bright morning sunlight of fall.

Jesse rolled down his window. "Hey, Melanie! Do you want a ride?" he called into the brisk air.

She stopped walking and turned to face him, her light green eyes as surprised as if she'd just that second become aware of his presence.

Jesse had to suppress a flash of irritation. What did she want him to think? That she and her dad had so many other red BMWs tooling up and down their private road that she didn't normally notice them?

"I thought you were suspended," she said.

"I'm pretty sure they can't suspend me from my own car," he shot back. "Unless, of course, you'd *rather* ride the bus."

The truth was he was grounded as well as suspended. And even though he had risked sneaking out of his house that Tuesday morning specifically to see Melanie, he had no intention of telling her that.

She yanked his passenger door open and dropped into the black leather seat. "What I meant was, why are you going to school?"

Her new position left a flawless stretch of

tan thigh exposed between the top of her cream-colored stockings and the hem of her short skirt. Any other day the sight would have left him unable to think about anything else, but that morning he took it in with the same numb lack of interest he felt in the rest of his life.

"I'm not going to school," he told her, making a U-turn back to the main road. "I was just out driving around, so I thought I'd cruise by. That's all."

Melanie raised her eyebrows, obviously aware he was lying. Oh well. He hadn't really expected her to believe that lame story anyway.

"Does, uh—does everyone in Eight Prime know what happened?" he asked.

"What do you think? The entire school knows." There wasn't the slightest trace of sympathy in her expression.

Jesse took one hand off the steering wheel and massaged his pounding forehead. He'd suspected as much, but it was still hard to hear. On the other hand, that's why he'd come to Melanie. He'd known she wouldn't pull any punches to spare his feelings. Not Melanie.

"So then I guess everyone thinks I'm an idiot for getting caught with liquor in my locker?"

Melanie shrugged, her tight lips making it clear that that was her opinion, at least.

"Listen, Melanie, do you think you could cut me some slack? Do you think I don't *know* what a moron I am? I've barely slept at all since I got busted Friday night. Believe me, I've had plenty of time to figure it out."

"Well, you *are* a moron. Do you have a drinking problem or what?"

"No, I don't have a problem—"

"Then why have liquor at school, Jesse?"

"It was just—"

"And what about getting drunk at that party and making an idiot of Nicole? Or how about after the Cave Creek game, when I had to . . ."

Slap you, Jesse supplied mentally, wondering what had stopped her from saying it.

"I think you do have a problem," she concluded.

"Like you're such an expert," he scoffed. What did Melanie know about drinking problems, anyway?

"If you don't want my opinion, why did you ask me?"

"I didn't ask you *that*."

"Fine." Melanie crossed her arms over the front of her red coat and they rode a few minutes in silence. By that point Jesse wished he could drop the whole subject, but there was one more thing he had to find out.

"Do the Junior Explorers know?" he asked finally. "Has anyone told Jason?"

The question seemed to take her by surprise. There was actually a hint of compassion in her voice when she said, "No, I don't think so. I don't see why anyone would tell them."

"I don't want Jason to know. I just . . . I'm quitting Eight Prime. Could you tell Peter for me?"

"*What?*" The sympathy of a moment before vanished. "No, I won't tell Peter for you. Tell him yourself, you big quitter!"

"Oh, that's mature—" Jesse began. They were pulling up to the curb in front of the high school.

"And I suppose bailing out on someone you've promised to help is all grown-up!" Melanie said furiously. "You make me sick!"

"Melanie, I—"

"I'm not talking to you!" She threw her car door open and sprang out onto the grass, slamming the heavy metal behind her.

"Great," Jesse muttered, watching her stalk off. Her back was stiff with indignation and her chin was high in the air. "That's just great."

The previous Friday, before all this had happened, he and Melanie had finally started making up a little. Now everything was ruined again. The thought made him feel like garbage.

He tore his gaze from Melanie and rolled back into traffic. As depressing as it was, Melanie being angry with him was not his biggest problem. Even the fact that now he'd have to talk to Peter himself was only a flea bite compared to the rest of it.

11

At home, Jesse's father was as mad as Jesse had ever seen him. Not only had he grounded Jesse for the length of his suspension, every time he laid eyes on him he'd assign another five feats of manual labor. Worse, Jesse was supposed to meet with Coach Davis after practice the next day to learn his fate with regard to football. Being suspended from classes for a week—that was nothing. But if he got cut from the *team* . . .

Jesse shuddered. He didn't think he could live with that.

"I want to talk to Jenna," Leah told Miguel, pointing across the quad. Jenna was sitting at a favorite outdoor table with Peter Altmann and Ben Pipkin, two other members of Eight Prime. "I want to see if she's heard anything from Jesse."

Miguel nodded and they threaded their way through the lunchtime crowd at the high school.

"Hi, you guys," Ben bellowed before they were twenty feet away. "How's it going?"

Leah smiled a greeting. Ben's goofy behavior didn't embarrass her most of the time, but she could sense Miguel cringing at her side. "Hi, Ben," she said, grabbing a seat at the table. Miguel remained standing behind her. "Has anyone heard from Jesse?"

Peter and Jenna shook their heads.

"We don't know anything new, then?" Leah asked.

"Well . . . he's still suspended," Ben offered helpfully.

"No kidding," Miguel muttered. Leah turned her head to shoot him a warning look. Maybe it was her imagination, but Miguel seemed even moodier that Tuesday than usual.

"I wonder if one of us ought to call him," Jenna mused. "I was kind of hoping he'd call us."

"Yeah," said Peter. "I've been going back and forth with that too. On the one hand, I'd like to make sure he's okay, but on the other, I don't want to embarrass him. Maybe he's not ready to talk about it yet."

"It's got to be hard for him," Miguel put in. "The guy practically lives for football."

"I think we should call him," Jenna said. "It's got to be better to call and maybe embarrass him a little than to let him think we don't care. Right?"

"What are we talking about?" asked a chipper new voice behind Leah. "Has anyone heard from Jesse?"

Leah turned again to see Nicole Brewster standing next to Miguel. Her best friend, Courtney Bell, was at her side. The only member of Eight Prime missing now was Melanie—and Jesse, of course.

"No one knows anything new," Leah told her. "We were just trying to decide if one of us ought to call him."

"I'll do it," Nicole offered immediately. "We

13

definitely ought to call and let Jesse know we support him, that we're behind him one hundred percent."

"Well . . . I don't know how much we *support* him," Jenna said slowly, her eyebrows drawn into a frown. "I mean, we sure don't condone what he did. I just thought we ought to tell him we're still his friends."

"Right," said Peter. "Everyone makes a mistake sometime."

"Getting caught with liquor in your locker is a bigger mistake than most," Miguel said.

Nicole slid into a seat beside Leah. "But don't you see? That's the only difference!" Her voice rang with conviction. "Everybody drinks. Jesse was just unlucky enough to get caught!"

"Or stupid enough," Leah heard Courtney mutter behind her.

"I don't drink," Peter said.

"Me either," said Jenna. "I mean, I wouldn't have anything against it if we were old enough, but we're not. Not only that, but Jesse broke school rules—"

"Oh, *please*!" Nicole interrupted. "You can't be serious. Everyone breaks the rules."

"I don't," said Peter.

"Me either," Jenna echoed.

"I could have told you *that*," Leah thought she heard Courtney whisper.

"Ben . . . ," Nicole began, looking to him for backup. She suddenly seemed to realize she was taking her case to the biggest nerd at school. "Never mind. Leah—"

"Oh, no. I'm not getting in the middle of this," Leah said hurriedly.

"Don't look at me," said Miguel.

Nicole seemed astonished. Her amazingly blue eyes were even wider than usual. "You've all got to be kidding me," she said indignantly.

"Look, Nicole," said Peter, "we have different opinions about what Jesse did, but that's not really important. What's done is done, and I'm sure he regrets it. We only want him to know that we aren't sitting around judging him for it."

"It sounds like you're judging him to me!" Nicole cried.

"Maybe I should make the phone call," Leah offered. "I think I know what to say."

"No! I'll do it," Nicole insisted. "I know what to say. I'll just tell him that we miss him, and that we're all still his friends. All right? Can everyone agree on that, at least?"

"Sure. That sounds nice," Jenna answered for them all.

"Okay, then." Nicole stood up just as the end-of-lunch bell rang. "I'll call him after school."

Everyone else grabbed their things and scattered on their way to fifth-period classes, but Leah and Miguel headed toward the main building together.

"Gee, our favorite class," Leah griped as they

15

walked. "Biology for the Brain Dead, with the multi-talented Ms. Walker."

Miguel chuckled. "Give the poor woman a break. If she hadn't gotten you so upset that first week of school, you and I might never have met."

"You don't think so? Not even after all this time?"

"Probably not," Miguel answered seriously. "And besides, what would my chances be now? I mean, now that you're a U.S. Girl?"

Leah groaned. "Don't even," she warned. She had known it would come up sometime, but she hated even thinking about that stupid contest, let alone being teased about it. It was horrible, but assuming Jesse was going to get in trouble anyway, she was actually kind of glad he'd done it when he had. It had completely removed the attention from her. Everyone at school was so busy talking about Jesse being suspended and whether or not he'd be kicked off the Wildcats that no one except Eight Prime even seemed to know about the modeling contest.

"I'm going out with a model," Miguel singsonged, flipping her French braid playfully.

"I'm warning you, Miguel."

"Aw, come on, Leah. You ought to be proud. *I'm* proud, and I didn't even win."

The unintended ambiguity of his statement made Leah smile in spite of herself. "And all of Missouri can be thankful for that. I don't think you'd have done too well in the swimsuit competition."

"There was a swimsuit competition?" he returned excitedly. "You didn't tell me that!"

"I was kidding," she said, rolling her eyes. "Can we please change the subject?"

Miguel hesitated uncertainly, as if unsure whether she meant it. "You're not still thinking of dropping out of the finals, are you?" he asked. "That would be a big mistake. Forget that you'd break Nicole's heart—what about the scholarship?"

The scholarship. Leah almost groaned out loud.

After she'd inadvertently won the Missouri portion of the U.S. Girls model search, she'd come home determined to drop out of the January finals at the very first opportunity. She'd had every intention of calling the contest organizers first thing the following Monday morning and letting the runner-up take her place. Then, just for the heck of it, she'd read the load of literature they'd shoved into her arms right before she left the contest site in St. Louis.

Out of the fifty girls selected in the preliminary contests—one in each state—U.S. Girls was selecting five final winners to be their models in a national ad campaign. Leah could care less about having her picture in magazines and getting a lot of free nail polish, but she'd almost fallen off her bed when she'd found out what the real prize was.

The final five winners would get scholarships of fifteen thousand dollars per year. *Each.* For four years. That was serious money. She could go to any college in the country with that kind of money.

Leah was sure she'd never forget Nicole's reply when she'd called her to ask about it. "Nicole," she'd said, "did you know that the final five in this U.S. Girls thing get enormous scholarships?"

"Um, yeah," Nicole had answered. "I think so. But hey, did you see the part about the facials? Free facials every week for a *year*, and free haircuts and makeup, too! Is that the best, or what?"

Or what, Leah thought now, shaking her head. She liked Nicole, but they didn't seem to have much in common.

"No. I'm not dropping out," Leah told Miguel grimly. "Not yet, anyway."

They reached the doors to the main building. Miguel pushed one open and held it for her to pass. "I'm dating a model," he sang, just loudly enough for her ears only.

"Yeah, well . . . whoopee," Leah retorted. "I don't even want to go out with you if that's the only reason you're dating me."

"Luckily for me you know it isn't," Miguel returned, unperturbed. "Because I was dating you before you won."

"Yeah. Well, *you* know that . . . and *I* know that, but . . ." *who else is going to believe it?* she finished

18

miserably. *The whole school is going to think Miguel only likes me now because I won that stupid contest.*

"Is something the matter?" he asked, bending to see her face.

"I just wish . . . I wish . . . Nothing."

Why had they kept their relationship a secret so long, anyway?

Two

By the time Jenna got home that Tuesday, she had a hundred things on her mind.

"What a lousy day," she grumbled, climbing the stairs to her third-floor bedroom. Jesse was suspended, Miguel was still trailing Leah the way a dinghy trails a yacht, and ever since Peter had found out about her stupid crush on Miguel, things hadn't been the same between them. And that was just at school!

She pushed her bedroom door open and walked inside, hanging her backpack over her desk chair before she took a look around. Her new, completely private bedroom was as great as ever, but she couldn't enjoy it anymore. Not the big double bed, not the window with the treetop view and the lilac drapes, not the built-in desk and bookshelves or the braided-denim rug on the polished hardwood floor. The room had lost all its appeal Sunday night, when Jenna had finally learned what her older sister, Caitlin, had sacrificed to give it to her.

Jenna had always known Caitlin was shy. Anyone who talked to her for thirty seconds knew that.

But in her heart, Jenna had suspected her of being lazy, too. She had expected Caitlin to move out of the house practically the second she graduated from high school, the way her oldest sister, Mary Beth, had done. But when Caitlin hadn't moved, hadn't gone to college, and hadn't gotten a job, Jenna had grown impatient. After all, Caitlin's lack of initiative was the only thing standing in the way of Jenna having her own room. Or so she'd thought. Now she knew that Caitlin had been trying to get a job all along.

Jenna threw herself down on her bed. *She was trying all that time and I never even guessed. And now, because of me, she's given up and moved in with Sarah.*

It made Jenna miserable to imagine how her painfully shy sister must have suffered during all those dead-end interviews. When the whole sad story had finally come out on Sunday, Caitlin herself had said—no, had *sobbed*—that she always did horribly. Jenna didn't doubt it, but she also didn't doubt that her sister would be a good worker. She just needed someone to give her a chance.

"Yeah, like you did," Jenna muttered. If she had only minded her own business, Caitlin would still be living in her third-floor bedroom and looking for a job instead of rooming with a ten-year-old. Jenna's constant pushing was what had made her give up in despair.

Jenna flipped onto her stomach and dragged one

limp hand along the cool wood floor, as if trailing her fingers over the side of a boat. *I am a horrible, selfish person*, she thought. The knowledge didn't much cheer her up.

She was still trying to decide what to do when the sound of her mother's piano in the living room broke in on her thoughts. Mrs. Conrad had begun playing "Amazing Grace," one of Jenna's favorite hymns. Jenna hummed along in her head as her mother played downstairs.

> *Amazing grace, how sweet the sound,*
> *That saved a wretch like me.*
> *I once was lost, but now am found,*
> *Was blind, but now I see.*

"Of course!" Jenna exclaimed, sitting up. "That's it!" She'd been blind too, where Caitlin was concerned, but now that she saw the problem clearly, she had a chance to redeem herself. Full of hope, Jenna jumped off her bed and ran down to the living room.

"Hi, Mom," she said, sliding in at the piano bench.

"Hi there." Mrs. Conrad kept playing without missing a beat, a legacy of practicing through all the trials and interruptions of raising six rowdy daughters. It was a useful skill for a choir director,

22

and one Reverend Thompson had taken note of when he'd hired her for the job. "What's up?"

"Nothing." Jenna took a deep breath, then rushed ahead. "Mom, did you know Caitlin was interviewing for jobs?"

"Of course." Her mother continued playing, but more softly. "Even if she hadn't told me, I'd have figured it out from the mail." Mrs. Conrad was referring to the numerous letters of rejection Caitlin had received from prospective employers.

"So why didn't you tell me?" Jenna demanded.

"Well, honey, it didn't seem like your business. I knew Caitlin wanted to tell everyone after she got a job, so that we could all be happy for her instead of feeling sorry."

"But if I'd known, I would have been more patient. Now everything is ruined."

The hymn came to an end. Mrs. Conrad took her fingers off the keys and turned to face her daughter. "I wish you had told me about your plan to swap rooms before you girls were already moving. If you'd come to me then, like you should have, I might have been able to talk Caitlin out of it."

"I know," Jenna said miserably. "I should have told you. But isn't there anything I can do to make it right now? I've offered to switch back probably five different times, but Caitlin won't do it. I feel just awful."

Mrs. Conrad smiled sadly. "I'm afraid you're going to feel awful a little longer then. Caitlin wants to punish herself for failing and you gave her a way to do it. I'm glad you offered her her old room back, but if she won't take it, you can't make her. The best thing to do is just be nice to her and let her find her own way. This won't last forever."

"But I promised I'd help her!"

"Then be her friend, Jenna, not just her sister. I'm telling you the truth—that's the best help you can give her."

Melanie stood beside the wall of windows in her mother's art studio, watching the world outside. It was a wild fall day, with a cold wind blowing loose leaves around. From her place behind the plate glass, they swirled and skittered silently, but Melanie knew that outside, the noise those dead leaves made would be surprisingly loud, especially when the wind roared through the treetops, shaking down new victims.

Blustery, she thought. *That's what it is.*

And something about the restlessness of the weather spoke to the same restlessness in her soul.

She backed indecisively away from the windows, then turned and hurried out of the studio, closing the door behind her. A moment later she was trotting down the Andrewses' gray marble staircase and grabbing a hooded parka out of the entryway closet.

She pulled it on over the sweater and jeans she'd changed into after school and opened her heavy front door.

"Bye, Dad," she called over her shoulder before a gust of wind blasted her in the face, nearly ripping the door from her fingers. She hung on somehow until the squall had passed, then shut the door quickly, leaning back against it until she heard the latch click.

She had decided to walk through the fields and woods to the creek on her back acres, and she set off now, her cheeks prickling in the chill blowing in from the north. It seemed she could almost feel the thermometer dropping as she made her way around the house to the open land behind it. She flipped her hood up over her hair, pulling the fluffy fur edging down low on her forehead. The fur smelled musty but familiar, comforting. She turned her head and snuggled her icy nose into it as she reached the beginning of the path through the fields.

The path wasn't used very often these days. There'd been a time when Melanie had walked to the creek nearly every afternoon, especially during the summer. She'd had a fort down there then, and a million friends, and the trail had been stamped wide and smooth by the footsteps of so many passings. Now dry grasses bent into her route, whipping against her denim-clad calves and tangling her booted feet. In the field all around her, the grass tossed and heaved with the bitter wind, flattening stalks that snapped back a moment later. She threw her arms wide and shouted, exhilarated by the power of the gale.

The sky was slowly filling with clouds. Thick gray banks loomed in every direction. But directly overhead, it was clear straight up to the sun. Rays of sunlight streamed down through the gap, throwing the fields at her feet into sharp, hard-shadowed relief. She hurried her steps anyway, afraid it might rain before she got home.

By the time she reached the edge of the woods, the sky was completely gray. Wind gusted all around her, tossing the branches over her head and releasing a confetti of colored leaves that blew and fluttered to the ground. She turned and glanced back toward the field just as a single bright shaft of sunlight broke dramatically through the clouds, washing a tawny swath of autumn grasses.

Hey, it's my painting! she thought, surprised into immobility by the familiarity of the scene. *The one I painted for Peter.* The details were different, but the effect—the feeling—was the same. *Exactly* the same.

Eerily the same.

Melanie felt a strange tingling sensation start over her heart and radiate down both arms. She hugged her ribs and shuddered, trying to shake it off.

So what? she thought. *Of course it looks like my painting—this is the field I painted.* But she'd been facing the other direction at the time, and the light hadn't been so dramatic then. Another shiver worked down her body. Melanie turned from the scene and headed more deeply into the trees.

She could barely hear the sound of water up ahead through the caterwauling wind. A minute later she stepped into a clearing. The creek burbled and splashed in its stony bed, tumbling over a small waterfall. Melanie wandered to the bank and sat on a rock to watch it, but her mind was still wrestling with what she'd seen in the field. It had all seemed so familiar. . . .

My accident! she thought suddenly. *Of course!* After she'd injured her head in the cheerleading stunt, her mind had been as full of light and shadow as the field. At first her darkness had been impenetrable, absolute. But, strangely, she hadn't been afraid. The whole time she'd drifted through unconsciousness, she'd felt safe . . . protected . . . not alone. When the unwelcome light of reality had broken in, scattering her mental clouds, she hadn't wanted to wake up.

"That's what I painted for Peter!" she exclaimed softly. She hadn't realized it at the time, but she was positive now. The light, the darkness . . . What she'd thought was an autumn field had actually been the contents of her own muddled head.

She shook that part of her anatomy now, reaching around to feel the stubbly place they'd shaved to stitch her up. Her hair was growing back, but the spot still felt weird and prickly, a concrete reminder of an experience she could otherwise almost believe she'd imagined—especially the part right before she'd become fully conscious, when she'd thought she'd seen her mother in the room.

Every time she remembered that moment, she was filled with new confusion. She couldn't believe she'd dreamed it, but what other explanation was there? Peter had said her apparition could have been an angel. Knowing Peter, that didn't surprise her. What surprised her was that she was actually considering his theory.

"What's happening to me?" she muttered, burying her cold hands deep in her pockets and huddling inside her parka. She felt completely recovered from her injury, but she still didn't feel normal. Ever since she'd woken up, she'd felt so strange, as if she were right on the edge of understanding something important.

Or maybe the change she perceived had started before her accident, and her injury had just sharpened the focus.

Yes, I think that's it, she decided, raising her eyes from the waterfall.

Because now that she was concentrating, Melanie was pretty sure she knew exactly when her strange, something's-about-to-change feeling had begun.

It was the day they had formed Eight Prime.

"Yeah, yeah. I'm coming," Leah muttered, wrestling the newspaper off her lap and heading for the kitchen. The telephone continued to ring insistently. "I said all right, already!"

She reached the old wall phone and grabbed the receiver off the hook. "Hello?"

"Leah? Leah, it's Nicole. Are you watching TV?"

"Well, actually—"

"Turn to channel twelve. Hurry!"

"Nicole, the television isn't on, and even if it were, I couldn't reach it. What's up?"

"What's up? You're on the news, that's all! Channel twelve is—"

But Leah didn't wait to hear more. "I'll call you back," she promised, hanging up. Charging into the living room, she dove for the remote and hurriedly flipped to channel twelve.

"Oh, no!" she gasped as the picture filled the screen. Someone had taped her victory walk at the U.S. Girls competition, complete with two dozen red-white-and-blue-ribboned roses and the goofy rhinestone tiara they'd made her wear and then give back.

"I'm so humiliated," she groaned, covering her face. "Everyone at school is going to see this!"

29

"Local beauty Leah Rosenthal took St. Louis by storm in the U.S. Girls national model search held there this past weekend," the news anchor's voice droned over the pictures.

"By *storm?*" Leah repeated, peering through her fingers. "Oh, please, just shoot me now."

"The winsome seventeen-year-old student from Clearwater Crossing High School is said to have held the audience breathless."

"*Who* said that?" she demanded of the screen. "What bull!" Then she groaned again. "Winsome. I am *dead*."

"Everyone here on the channel twelve news team wishes Leah the best of luck this January, when she'll compete in California against the preliminary winners from all fifty states. You go, girl!"

"Aargh," Leah groaned, flipping off the set and throwing herself backward into the sofa cushions. So much for keeping a low profile at school—her cover was totally blown! Now everyone was going to tease and embarrass her and make a big deal. Why had she ever let Nicole talk her into entering that stupid contest in the first place?

The phone rang again. Leah had a pretty good idea who was calling.

"Wasn't that outrageous?" Nicole cried the second Leah picked up the line. "I got most of it on tape, if you want a copy. I can't wait for school tomorrow—everyone's going to be so excited! I know you said you didn't want us to spread it around, but since the whole town just saw it on the news, I guess we can talk about it now, right?"

Leah opened her mouth to answer, but Nicole was wound tighter than a drugstore perm.

"I didn't even know they had TV cameras there. Did you? I mean, I guess it could have been home video, but the picture was really good. *You* looked *great!* I wish they'd shown your first walk, though, because that was the one I missed. If they hadn't made us all—"

"Nicole—"

"—stand behind that stupid stage, then I might have been able to see you. That was really kind of dumb, when you think about it. There wasn't any reason—"

"Nicole—"

"—to keep us all back there. They could have let us sit in the audience after we'd had our turn. Then we'd at least have gotten to see some of the other contestants. All I got to see was the back of that stupid stage, and—"

"Nicole! There's someone on call-waiting. Can't you hear that clicking? I have to get that. It might be one of my parents."

"Okay. I'll hold."

"Uh . . . okay." Leah had hoped to end the call, but there wasn't time to argue. She hurriedly pressed the button to connect the second line. "Hello?"

"May I speak to Leah Rosenthal, please?" a woman asked in cultivated—overly cultivated—tones.

"This is Leah."

"Oh, splendid. Leah, my name is Kristell Lawrence."

"Kris*tell*?" Leah repeated.

"Exactly. I'm the director of marketing for U.S. Girls, St. Louis. The reason I'm calling, dear, is to give you some *wonderful* news. The Missouri U.S. Girls stores are *so* excited about our new campaign, and they really like your look. We want you to do a photo shoot this Thursday for some local advertising. Isn't that great?"

"I go to school on Thursdays."

Kris*tell* laughed. "Of course you do, dear. We're not completely inexperienced with this sort of thing, you know. Now listen, I have it all set up. Do you have a little something to write on?"

Leah found a pen and pad on the counter. "Yes."

"Good." Kristell gave her the address of a photo studio downtown. "Now, they're expecting you at four. That should give you plenty of time to get there after school. Be sure to bring a white T-shirt and blouse, and some solid shirts in bright colors. They'll have the jeans, of course, but I don't know what they'll want you to wear on top. Maybe nothing!"

"I am *not*—"

"It was a joke, dear. Kidding! Anyway, I've got to fly. Congratulations, and have a great time Thursday." The line clicked dead.

"Of all the nerve!" Leah sputtered. "She never even asked if I'd do it!"

"Do what?" Nicole asked eagerly.

Leah squeezed her eyes shut, took a deep breath, and counted to three. She'd totally forgotten Nicole was holding on the other line.

"That was some woman named Kristell, if you can believe that. U.S. Girls is having a stupid photo shoot on Thursday and she basically just called me up and ordered me to be there. She didn't even ask if I wanted to go."

"Oh, Leah!" Nicole exclaimed. "Oh wow! How exciting!"

Leah didn't reply. She didn't want to offend Nicole, but they didn't see eye-to-eye on this modeling thing at all.

"Can I go?" Nicole begged. "Oh, *please*. Say yes," she added in a rush. "I'll stay out of the way and I won't be a pest and I'll—"

"They didn't say anything about bringing a friend," Leah interrupted before Nicole got too carried away.

"Then they didn't say you *couldn't* bring one, right? Oh, please, Leah. Please? I've never seen a photo shoot before."

33

Leah considered. If bringing Nicole made the U.S. Girls people mad, what did she care? She wasn't too happy with them at the moment, either. Besides, if she had to do this stupid thing, *someone* might as well enjoy it.

"Okay, why not? It'll be good to have a friend along."

"Oh, thanks!" gushed Nicole. "This is going to be so cool! Do you want to borrow anything? I have tons of hair clips and headbands and things like that. Hey! I could help you do your hair if you want! And your makeup! I didn't want to say anything before, but you wore hardly any at the contest. For photos they're going to want more. Have you seen that new look on the runway models, with the jewel-toned eye shadows up the eyebrow? I'll grant you, it's a little much for everyday, but . . ."

Leah set the phone down on the counter and rubbed her aching temples. Even from that distance she could hear Nicole chattering on and on, oblivious to the fact that no sound came from the other end. Leah had never heard Nicole talk so much, let alone so fast.

What have I agreed to? she thought with a moan, rubbing her temples again.

From the desk of Principal Kelly
(Teachers: Please read in homeroom.)

Good morning, students.

The football game this week is an away game against the Mapleton Mavericks. I know many of you won't be able to travel the distance to the game, so I encourage you all to support your team by participating in our Spirit Day on Friday. Remember to wear your green and gold!

And speaking of football, one of the biggest events of the school year is not that far away. The CCHS homecoming game and bonfire will be held Friday night, November 6th, with the homecoming dance taking place the following night, on Saturday. The dance is a formal and open to all grade levels. Come with a date or by yourself, but definitely plan to come.

Go, Wildcats!

Three

Mrs. Wilson finished reading the principal's memo and looked up at Jenna's first-period geometry class.

"I can't believe it's homecoming time already!" the teacher exclaimed. "The semester's just flying by!"

"Yeah, for *you*," Jenna's friend, Cyn Girard, muttered under her breath.

Jenna smiled, putting her hand over her mouth so the teacher wouldn't notice.

"It's not like it's happening tomorrow," a boy in the front row pointed out. "It's still almost three weeks away."

"It will be here before you know it," Mrs. Wilson predicted. "That's how these things go. Now, take out your books and open to page ninety-three."

Groans and a reluctant pawing through backpacks followed. Jenna's book was already open on her desk, so she used the wasted interval to sneak a good look at Miguel. He was sitting in his usual place, one row over to her right. With a twinge, Jenna remembered how excited she'd been to see him take that seat on the very first day of school. It was hard to believe now, but at the time she'd been deluded enough to think he might finally notice her.

I wonder if he and Leah will go to the homecoming dance together, she mused. *They won't be able to keep up the "just friends" act if they do.*

A second later, however, she had to rethink that conclusion. She and Peter had been going to dances together since sixth grade—and there certainly wasn't a romance there.

We're getting kind of old to keep doing that, though. Especially now that we're juniors. And homecoming is a formal. We ought to have dates by now.

The whole situation was depressing. And the more Jenna thought about it, the more depressed she became. She could see it all in her head in crystal-clear detail: Leah and Miguel, dressed like the cover people they were, arm in arm, dancing every slow dance. . . . she and Peter, standing around, sipping sticky pink punch like reject throwbacks to junior high. . . .

How humiliating. Maybe I won't even go.

"So! Finally I get you alone!" Miguel teased, dropping onto the grass beside Leah.

His tone was light, but to keep it that way was an effort. All morning long, everyone on campus had seemed to be trying to talk to Leah. People who didn't even know her—who had never noticed her or said hello before—had seen her on the news and were acting like her new best friends. It was ridiculous. He'd tried to get a minute alone with her between classes twice and both times it had been impossible.

"Oh, right. Like I'm enjoying this," Leah retorted. "Do you know that some girl I never met before started talking to me in the hall, followed me into the girls' room, and practically came into my stall? I had to shut the door in her face, and she just stood there talking anyway."

"Ah, the trials of the rich and famous," Miguel said, leaning slightly into her shoulder. It was a risk—they never touched in public—but he couldn't help himself. With everyone suddenly trying to get between them, he wanted the reassurance of physical contact. He was glad that Leah had won the contest, and he certainly didn't begrudge her the attention. He just didn't want to be forgotten in all the confusion.

"I'm hardly rich or famous." Leah inclined her head toward his. "But I *do* feel like I'm on trial. It seems like everyone's checking me out every second. What I'm doing, what I'm wearing . . ."

"I love what you're wearing," Miguel told her. He wasn't exactly an expert on women's clothing, but he had noticed that Leah wore a lot of skirts. Today she had on a long, soft pink floral one, along with a darker pink top and a short, baby pink sweater over that. The color brought out the glow in her cheeks, while the layered style emphasized her height. "Probably five or six different girls are going to show up at school in that exact same outfit tomorrow."

Leah groaned. "Don't even *think* that. I'm just . . . not ready for this, Miguel. I don't mean to sound conceited or ungrateful, but I never thought I'd be doing something so—"

"Hey! Hi, guys!" shouted a voice right behind them.

They immediately snapped bolt upright, their private moment shattered. And even though Miguel knew instantly who their stalker was, his heart still pounded from the surprise.

"Hello, Ben," said Leah.

"I've been looking for you everywhere!" Ben complained, dropping cross-legged onto the grass in front of them. "I saw you on TV, Leah. And everyone's talking about you in all of my classes. How come when you told me about the contest you made it sound like it wasn't a big deal?" Ben's eyes held a slightly wounded look behind their thick glasses.

"I didn't want it to be."

"But it *is*." Ben turned from Leah to appeal to Miguel. "Isn't it?"

"Apparently so," Miguel said dryly.

"There you are, Leah!" cried Nicole. Miguel looked up to see her barreling toward them across the small lawn behind the cafeteria. "I've been searching all over for you!"

Join the club, Miguel thought, struggling to keep a sense of humor.

Nicole dropped onto the grass between Ben and Leah. "Look. Look what I brought you," she said, ignoring the guys completely as she forced a ripped-out magazine page on Leah. "*That's* what I was talking about yesterday. See how they do that with the eye shadow?"

"Hey! Hey, Miguel!" came another greeting from across the lawn. Three of Miguel's friends from the water polo team were headed toward them too.

"Hi, Derrick . . . Mike . . . Roger," Miguel said, but they were barely even aware of him. All three pairs of eyes were glued to Leah.

"Hi, there!" Derrick said, interrupting Nicole's steady stream of chatter to flash Leah a leering smile. Derrick Spalding was a wolf. Everyone who knew him knew he couldn't be trusted with girls. His disrespectful behavior had never made much of an impression on Miguel before, but that day he felt a sudden urge to jump up and punch Derrick out.

"I didn't know you knew this guy," Derrick flirted with Leah, directing a cursory nod toward Miguel.

"I didn't know I knew you," Leah said, clearly

unimpressed. Mike and Roger laughed, and Miguel relaxed a little.

Derrick was undeterred. "That's exactly the oversight I'm here to correct."

"Hi. I'm Mike," Mike broke in before Leah could respond. "And this is Roger. We're all friends of Miguel's. Hey, congratulations on that contest thing."

"Thanks," Leah murmured, "but I think it was a fluke."

"Oh, no way!" Mike protested. "I saw you on the news. You were awesome."

Leah flushed and looked away.

"So, do you do a lot of modeling?" Roger asked.

Unlike Derrick, Mike and Roger were both pretty decent guys. Miguel was sure they'd never be hitting on Leah if they knew he was dating her. The problem was, they didn't. *No one* did. What had started out as a fun little secret between the two of them was turning into a world-class nightmare. Suddenly Leah was the hottest thing on campus and, as far as anybody knew, completely and totally single. The thought made Miguel slightly queasy. If he didn't make it known that he was her boyfriend soon, he could be replaced before he got the chance. It was definitely time to bring their romance out into the open. But how? He couldn't exactly run around school telling everyone Leah was his girlfriend.

41

The homecoming dance! he thought, nailing the perfect solution. He'd take Leah to the dance, and when they got there they'd be a couple for all the world to see. By the end of the night, the whole school would know they were together without him actually having to tell anybody. The solution appealed to him immensely. *The dance isn't that far away. Let's see. It's Wednesday now, so that's two and a half more weeks.* It was a little farther off than he would have liked, but otherwise the plan was ideal. Should he risk waiting?

Sure, he decided. *Why not? We've waited this long. We ought to last for a couple more weeks.* The matter settled in his mind, he began paying attention to the conversation again.

Leah was still trying to explain to Mike and Roger that she wasn't actually a model, and Derrick was still checking her out. Miguel leaned back on his elbows, determined to wait out the present assault without displaying any hint of displeasure. After all, Leah was a beautiful girl—it was only natural that his friends would give it a try. He wasn't worried.

Not very, anyway.

I'll get her alone later and asked her to the dance, he thought. *Maybe we can drive up to the lake after school.* He smiled at the thought of the two of them all alone in their favorite spot, Leah snuggling into his arms for protection against the cool fall air. He could imagine the green lake water,

Leah with just the slightest rippling of goose bumps on her arms, his bulky brown sweater keeping them both warm.

The end-of-lunch bell rang. "Oops! There's the bell!" Leah exclaimed, jumping to her feet. "Got to go!"

The group seemed reluctant to break up, but Leah swung her backpack onto her shoulders and strode off toward the main building without a backward glance.

"We have biology together now. See ya," Miguel explained quickly before he hurried to catch up.

He finally caught her in the hall. "Could you walk a little faster?" he complained. "I'm not quite sprinting yet."

"Sorry," she said, slowing her long steps. "I just had to get out of there."

"Tell me about it! Today's been a total drag."

Leah shrugged and looked away.

"How about we go to the lake after school?" he suggested. "I've got something I want to ask you."

"Can't you ask me here?"

Miguel glanced around the packed hallway and shook his head. "I'd rather ask you there."

Leah sighed. "Well, I can't go. I've got a stupid photo shoot for U.S. Girls tomorrow after school. That means that this afternoon I have to get ahead on my homework, figure out what clothes to—"

"Leah, that's great!" he interrupted, excited.

43

"What are the pictures for? Why didn't you tell me before?"

"I don't know what the pictures are for. Some ad," she said, making a sour face. "And I didn't tell you before because I'm not too happy about it. I don't even want to do it, if you want to know the truth. This whole modeling thing is stressing me out, Miguel."

She *did* look pretty stressed out. Still, Miguel couldn't believe that Leah didn't want to do the shoot. *I'll bet she's just nervous*, he thought.

"You're going to do great," he reassured her. "I'm so proud of you."

Leah gave him crooked smile. "Yeah. Whatever," she said weakly.

"So. What do you have to say for yourself?" Coach Davis asked.

Jesse shifted uncomfortably in the cold wooden chair. *You knew he'd ask something like that*, he told himself unhappily. *If you had half a brain, you'd have made up a speech before you got here*. He could barely meet the coach's eyes across his cluttered desk as he strained to think of a reply. *If I had half a brain, I wouldn't even be here*, was the only thing that came to mind.

"Nothing," he muttered at last, staring at his shoes. "I know I blew it."

"Do you?" asked the coach. "Aren't you going

to tell me why you did it? Don't you have a good reason?"

Jesse looked up, bewildered. "What good reason could there be? I mean, sure, I had reasons. But I'm guessing you won't want to hear them. I just shouldn't have done it, that's all."

Coach Davis gave him a long, hard look, then smiled and leaned back in his chair. "Bravo, Jones. I guess you're smarter than I thought."

Jesse flinched at the insult, but deemed it safest to return his gaze to the floor.

"I'm not stupid, you know, Jones," the coach went on. "And I'm certainly not so naïve as to believe that none of my players drinks. I was a teenager once too. I can guess what goes on at those parties. But drinking on campus—keeping a bottle in your locker—that's something else entirely. I'm afraid you have a problem."

Jesse's teeth clenched with annoyance. So he had a few drinks here and there. Why was everyone intent on giving him a drinking problem? He opened his mouth to argue, then shut it abruptly. If he made Coach Davis any madder, he *would* have a problem.

"Oh, good decision, Jones." The coach applauded facetiously. "You're showing definite potential here."

Jesse clamped his jaw shut tighter, determined not to react.

"You know, I could kick you off the team right now. A lot of coaches would."

Jesse nodded stiffly. He didn't doubt it a bit.

"And maybe I ought to, too. But I haven't made up my mind."

Then there was still a chance!

"I know I blew it, Coach," Jesse said hurriedly, eager to make the most of the coach's indecision. "But if you give me another chance, I swear I won't let you down. I *live* for football. Please, *please* let me back on the team."

The coach tilted forward in his chair and leaned his elbows on the desk. "I'll think about it," he said slowly, his eyes fixed intently on Jesse.

Jesse felt suddenly like an ant with a magnifying glass between it and the sun. It took every bit of his self-control to return the coach's gaze without squirming.

"When do you come back to classes? Monday?"

Jesse nodded.

"Well, don't bother coming to practice. I couldn't face myself in the mirror if I didn't keep you out for at least two games. That means no Mapleton next week, and you're out for homecoming, too. You're not going to practice, suit up, sit on the bench—anything. And I'm not promising I'll take you back after homecoming, understand? I'll reevaluate your status—that's all."

"I understand," Jesse said somehow. The disap-

46

pointment of missing homecoming was almost over-whelming. Only the knowledge that things could have gone a lot worse helped him keep his outward composure. "And I appreciate your not just kicking me off right now. No one would have blamed you for it . . . not even me."

Coach Davis chuckled. "Jones, if you'd been half this bright when you were still on the team, we wouldn't be sitting here now. But be sure you *do* understand. Your not drinking anymore is my condition for letting you back on the Wildcats. And that means giving up drinking completely—at parties, on the sly, wherever. One more slip and you'll never get back on this team."

Jesse nodded his agreement to all of the coach's conditions. But by the time he got back outside, he was already starting to resent them.

I can't believe I'm out for homecoming, he thought disgustedly, swinging into the driver's seat of his BMW. *And Mapleton won't be an easy win, either— the team could really use me.* He started his car and tore out of the lot, the fact that he had miraculously avoided being cut from the team already completely overshadowed by his irritation at missing two major games. Then he realized there were only two games left between homecoming and the finals, and he got even more upset.

The whole thing sucks. And like I'm really going to give up drinking! I mean, sure, at school, and before

47

games and stuff. But completely? What would be the point? Now I'm just going to have to sneak around like a criminal and make sure nothing gets back to the coach.

Which reminded him that he still hadn't told Peter he was quitting Eight Prime. Not only that, but there was a meeting at Nicole's the next night.

Nicole had phoned him at home after school on Tuesday, and even though he was supposedly grounded, Elsa had let him take the call. It would have actually been less punishment if his stepmother had told Nicole he wasn't allowed to talk. Nicole had been oozing misplaced worry and concern. She had also been nervous, talking so fast he had barely been able to get a word in. He'd known she was trying to cheer him up, but sympathy was the last thing he wanted. Especially from her.

"Everyone is completely behind you," she'd said. "One hundred percent. Except, well . . . maybe Peter and Jenna don't think people should drink before they turn twenty-one, but you know how they are. They mean well. They still *like* you. Leah and Miguel . . . well, they might have thought you shouldn't have brought alcohol to school—I'm not sure. It doesn't matter, though. We're all still really behind you!"

Yeah, right, Jesse thought bitterly as he drove toward home. *Sure you are.* It didn't matter anymore, though. He barely cared, in fact.

He just wished now that he'd told Nicole he was quitting Eight Prime. He should have. Maybe Melanie wouldn't tell Peter, but Nicole would have for sure.

"Nicole would do whatever I wanted," he muttered. The thought didn't cheer him up. What he needed was a friend, not a groupie.

For a moment, he considered calling one of his brothers. They were both away at college—Kevin at MIT and Steve at Princeton—but he knew they'd understand. Or they'd try to, anyway. They'd both moved away before Dr. Jones had remarried, so neither of them had experienced firsthand the thrill of living with Elsa and her spoiled-brat daughter, Brittany.

Jesse sighed. To be fair, it wasn't even that Elsa and Brittany were so *very* horrible. It was just that . . . *This isn't the way things were supposed to turn out.* That a diehard California kid like him had been exiled to the sticks of Misery was bad enough. But to be suspended from the football team in disgrace—he couldn't call his brothers and tell them that. He'd sound totally pathetic.

Besides, it wasn't as if the three of them were so close anymore. Once Kevin and Steve had gone off to college, they were *gone*. There hadn't been even a backward glance.

Jesse didn't blame them a bit.

Four

"Hi, you guys. Mind if I sit here?" Melanie asked.

Jenna and Peter looked up from their usual table. "Hi, Melanie," Jenna greeted her. "Sure, have a seat."

"How are you feeling?" Peter asked.

Melanie smiled as she slid into a seat beside him. "Fine. You mean, because of my head? If it weren't for that stubbly spot, you'd never even know it had happened."

"That, and you're still not cheering," Jenna pointed out.

Melanie nodded. "No, that's true. I'm sitting out the Mapleton game, but I'll start practicing again next week. I'll be back out there for homecoming."

"No more flips," Peter said, referring to the stunt that had caused her accident. "I don't think my heart could take another one of those ambulance rides."

His smile was wide, showing straight white teeth,

50

but his blue eyes were solemn beneath his blond bangs. Melanie wasn't sure if he was teasing or not. She felt awkward talking to him there, in front of Jenna. If they'd been alone, she might have teased back to see what he'd meant. Maybe she'd have said something like, "Most guys would kill to have me passed out in a car with them."

Or maybe not. Not to Peter. A comment like that would only embarrass him.

Which is why I like him so much, she thought, missing the times the two of them had spent together when she'd been recovering from her accident. It made her almost sorry to be well, because now the only times she got to see him were uncomfortable moments like these.

"No more flips," she agreed, opening her lunch. She took out an apple and bit in, wondering if Jesse had been man enough to tell Peter he was ditching Eight Prime. She was just about to ask when a guy dropped down beside her.

"There you are, Melanie!" senior Ricky Black said, sliding in so far on the bench that his thigh pressed up against hers. "I found you!"

"What do you want, Ricky?" she asked, moving away. Ricky was one of those guys who didn't take anything seriously—except maybe basketball. Whatever he was up to was bound to be something silly.

"Nice way to greet a friend!" He put on an

injured look. Ricky's expressions were always overdone to the point of really bad acting. "Aren't you even going to introduce me?"

"All right. Ricky, these are my friends Jenna Conrad and Peter Altmann. Jenna, Peter, meet Ricky Black. There. Now, what do you want?" she repeated.

Ricky smirked ingratiatingly at Peter and Jenna, then returned his attention to Melanie. "I love a woman who gets to the point," he purred suggestively.

"Yuck. You've got till the count of three. One . . . two . . ."

"You are *so* impatient. Actually, I'm thinking of taking you to the homecoming dance. How does that grab you?"

Melanie shrugged. "I'm underwhelmed."

"Is that your answer?" Ricky demanded, his heavy eyebrows raised.

"Believe it or not, Ricky, you don't just walk up to someone and *tell* her you're taking her to a dance. You're supposed to ask her if she'd like to go with you."

Ricky flashed a flirty smile. "I thought that was a foregone conclusion."

"Yeah, well, think again. Besides, I'm going with someone else."

"Oh." Ricky looked vastly disappointed—for exactly one second. "Then how about that model chick friend of yours? Leah What's-her-name. How about fixing us up?"

"You've got to be kidding. Anyway, I think she has a date." Melanie had promised Leah she wouldn't give away her secret relationship with Miguel, but she couldn't imagine that they wouldn't go to the dance together. "Hey, I know—why don't you ask one of the freshmen, Ricky? Someone who doesn't know you would probably *love* to be your date."

"And waste an honor like that on a freshman?" He shook his head. "All right, then, Melanie. I'm devastated, et cetera, et cetera, but it's your loss." He winked at her before he slid out of the table and sauntered off across the quad. "See you there."

Two more weeks of this, Melanie thought cheerlessly as she watched him go. It happened every time there was a dance. Ever since junior high school, guys had been rushing to ask her to these things, as if showing up with her were like bringing some kind of trophy. She couldn't even complain about it, because she knew how conceited it sounded. Even so, it wasn't fun being pressured by guy after guy, having to tell them all no, eventually settling on someone who seemed nice enough but who never turned out to be "the one."

Just once she wished there were someone she actually wanted to go with. Someone sweet . . . someone who actually liked her . . .

"Who are you going to the dance with, Melanie?" asked Jenna, practically reading her thoughts.

"What? Oh. I don't know. I don't have a date yet."

"But you just told Ricky you were going with someone else."

Melanie smiled. She hadn't made it this far without learning a trick or two. "And I am. If I go at all, that is. I hate formals. They're so stiff and fake and boring."

"But you *have* to go to homecoming," Jenna protested. "All the cheerleaders do."

"That's true," Peter said, smiling. "Besides, it won't be the same if you aren't there."

Melanie stifled a groan. Jenna was right—she'd have to go with someone.

But who?

"Leah, you should do this," Nicole advised from the sidelines, pursing her thin lips into a silly, pouty expression.

"Or not," Leah muttered. "Give me a break, Nicole."

"Fix your shirt," Nicole returned, motioning for Leah to pull the knot up higher on the goofy red gingham midriff they'd made her wear, despite the fact that she'd brought half the tops in her closet. Leah already felt like that ditsy blonde on

The Beverly Hillbillies—she didn't need more skin exposed between her blouse and her hip-hugging jeans.

"The shirt's fine," she said through gritted teeth.

They'd only been at the photo shoot an hour, and already she regretted bringing Nicole. So far all she'd done was pepper Leah with ridiculous suggestions and preen around in her skintight jeans, as if the judges were suddenly going to realize their heinous error and give the U.S. Girls title to her instead. Not that Leah cared—Nicole could have it with her blessing.

"Okay, dear, now you really have to keep still," the makeup woman told her, a slightly irritated edge to her voice. "Stop looking at your friend."

Make her stop looking at me, Leah wanted to say. But it wasn't just Nicole—everyone was looking at her. She felt like a freak in all the artificial poses the photographer wanted her to strike. Not to mention the hair and makeup people rushing over every few minutes and rearranging her as if she were a mannequin. She'd been combed and teased and sprayed half to death and they weren't even close to finished.

Her mother bent down to whisper in her ear. "Think of the scholarship," Mrs. Rosenthal advised. "Think of that, and just be yourself."

Whoever that was. A month before, Leah would have assumed she knew. Lately she wasn't so sure.

The Leah Rosenthal she knew would never have sold out this way, scholarship or no scholarship.

"Stanford. Harvard. Yale," her mother whispered, reading her mind.

"Yeah, all right," Leah whispered back, smiling slightly in spite of her irritation. She was glad her mother had come—Mrs. Rosenthal was the only sane person in the room.

"Okay, enough. That's marvelous," the photographer, Damón, declared, shooing everyone but Leah off the set.

"Okay, Leah. Now, real pouty, sweetheart. Real sexy. Go like this." He made the face Nicole had worn only seconds before. Nicole beamed and made it too, turning toward Damón to make sure he saw her.

Leah rolled her eyes. "I'm thinking I can't do that."

Damón lowered his camera a little. "Why not?"

"Because I'll feel like an idiot, that's why! I thought I was supposed to be a U.S. Girl—you know, like a regular, everyday person. Do you think I walk around school making those kinds of faces?"

Damón chuckled as if she were an amusing child. "This is theater, Leah. *Drama*. It's not real life."

You can say that again, Leah thought, scowling.

"Oh! Better!" cried Damón, snapping away like crazy. "That's even better! Let's go with that. Oh, excellent . . . perfect . . ."

Nicole looked startled for a moment, then started to scowl as well, bunching her blond brows fiercely over black-lined turquoise eyes. She tossed her heavily moussed hair to add to the effect, then glanced around to see if anyone was watching.

Leah was the only one who seemed to notice. *Poor Nicole*, she thought, shaking her head. *She would have loved to do this.*

"Yes! More!" urged Damón. "Toss that hair around."

Leah tossed, closing her eyes to hide her embarrassment.

"Oh, yes! I like that, too!" Damón shouted happily. His camera clicked and whirred with abandon.

Think of the scholarship, Leah told herself over and over again. *This could be your ticket to a fantastic new life.*

And it was then that she finally realized what the problem was—she had liked her *old* life just fine.

"Okay, I think I'm ready," Nicole announced to the empty basement room where the Thursday Eight Prime meeting was about to be held.

To get things set up in time, she'd had to rush home from Leah's photo shoot and run around like crazy, skipping dinner in favor of taking a shower and redoing her makeup. "I'll eat at the meeting," she'd told her mother. "We're having all that food."

Nicole studied her party setup now with a sense

of intense satisfaction. All her trouble had been worthwhile. Neither Peter nor Jenna had ever laid out the kind of spread Nicole had put together, and she'd decorated, too. Two folding tables had been set up on one side of the room and covered with paper tablecloths printed with leaves in harvest colors. On the first table, Nicole had placed a large metal tub full of ice, juice, and sodas. Next to that were plates, napkins, and plastic silverware. The second, longer table held a complete assortment of hors d'oeuvres so complete they were practically a meal. The usual chips, fruit, and cheeses were represented, but there were also a layer cake from the bakery, a bowl of macaroni salad, and the coup de grâce: two fancy silver chafing dishes filled with spicy chicken wings and her mom's famous barbecued meatballs.

This is the first time we've ever needed silverware, Nicole congratulated herself, nervously wiping her palms on the legs of her U.S. Girls jeans. Then she glanced down at the shirt she'd changed into and smiled. It was the same red-and-white gingham midriff Leah had worn for the shoot— the wardrobe girl had given it to Leah and, as soon as they were in the car, Leah had given it to her.

"Are you crazy?" Nicole had gasped. "You don't want it?"

"Do you like it?" Leah had countered. "Take it. I didn't want to insult anyone, but I'll never wear it again."

"Uh, th-thanks," Nicole had stammered, overwhelmed.

She gazed down at her prize now and hiked up the knot in front to expose more bare skin. Her U.S. Girls jeans were higher-waisted than the new style they'd given Leah to wear, so the effect with the top wasn't nearly as daring, but there was still a ribbon of flesh peeking out all the way around. She'd had to turn on the heat in the basement to get away with wearing a midriff, but was it ever going to be worth it. She couldn't wait for Jesse to see her!

More than that, she couldn't wait to see him. He'd been gone from school for so long she thought she might be in withdrawal.

"What are you having down here—a meeting or a wedding?" asked a sarcastic voice behind her. Nicole spun around to see her thirteen-year-old sister, Heather, walking down the basement stairs, her eyes on the elaborate snacks. "Oh, I get it. You *wish*, right?"

Nicole's hands went to her hips. "If you embarrass me in front of Jesse again, I swear to God I'll—"

"Mom!" Heather screamed happily. "Nicole's swearing!"

"Shut up, you little pain," Nicole hissed back. "Having a crush on your Sunday-school teacher doesn't make you any holier than anyone else, you know."

Heather turned white. She froze on the staircase, one step from the bottom.

"What's the matter, Heathen?" Nicole taunted. "You look positively pale."

Heather turned and fled back up the stairs just as the doorbell sounded.

Well, I guess I got rid of her! Nicole laughed to herself, ignoring the twinge of guilt she felt at exploiting her sister's one weakness. After all, hadn't Heather started it? With an effort, she forced the affair from her mind, especially the part about her swearing. No matter how hard she tried to be good, it seemed she was always tripping over things like that—low little things she didn't see until she'd already stubbed her toe.

Jenna and Peter appeared at the top of the staircase, Ben right behind them in a pair of too-huge jeans cinched below the rib cage with a skinny black leather belt. Nicole was getting used to Ben's weird outfits, but this time she couldn't help wondering if those were his father's pants or if he was going for that look on purpose.

Somehow she managed not to laugh. "Hi, you guys!" she called. "Come down and have some food."

The three of them tore into the buffet, Ben with so much enthusiasm that Nicole belatedly wished she'd made them wait until Jesse had seen it. Soon Leah arrived with Miguel, followed closely by Melanie. Miguel filled a plate with chicken and meatballs, while Leah picked at the fruit and cheese. Melanie looked the whole table over, then selected a diet soda.

How typical, thought Nicole, dropping her hands to her abdomen. The hard prominence of hipbones just beneath the denim reassured her, but she tugged nervously at the knot on her shirt anyway. "I wonder where Jesse is?" she said loudly. "He's a little late tonight."

Ben looked up from his chicken wings. "He's *real* late," he corrected with barbecue-sauce-covered lips. "Maybe he isn't coming."

Nicole's empty stomach compressed as if it had just dropped three floors in a runaway elevator. "Why wouldn't he be coming?"

Ben shrugged. "Well, he *is* suspended from school. If I ever got suspended, I'd be in so much trouble at home it wouldn't even be funny. Maybe his folks wouldn't let him come."

Ben's words made sense, but Nicole didn't want to believe him. "If he wasn't coming, he'd have called me," she insisted. "Or he could have told me when I talked to him on Tuesday."

She had to force herself not to wince at the

memory of that phone call. She'd been so nervous that she'd rambled like a fool, and after she'd hung up she'd been embarrassed to the point of actually crying. It was just so hard to talk to Jesse. He made it hard, somehow.

"I don't think Jesse's coming," Melanie said, walking over to the best chair in the room and dropping into its cushy seat. "We might as well start without him."

"What makes you say that?" asked Peter.

"I don't know," Melanie returned obscurely. "Has he talked to you at all?"

Peter shook his head. "No. I haven't seen him all week. Have you?"

"I just . . ." Melanie crossed her tan legs, then uncrossed them again. "I think we should start, that's all. If he shows up, he shows up."

Peter kept his eyes on Melanie. It seemed as obvious to him as it was to Nicole that she wasn't telling all she knew. He glanced at his watch. "It *is* getting late," he acknowledged.

Ben rushed to the couch with his plate and sat down. "Are we starting?" he asked eagerly. "I have big news!"

Everyone looked to Nicole. She wanted to scream *"No,"* that there wasn't any point to having a meeting without Jesse, but somehow she nodded without bursting into tears. "I guess so."

The rest of the group took seats on the furniture in the center of the room, but Nicole remained frozen beside the buffet.

Ben didn't seem to notice. "I got us a building for the haunted house!" he announced proudly. "My dad's company, ComAm, has an old storehouse down by the railroad tracks, and there's nothing in it right now. They said we can use it for our fund-raiser if we clean up afterward and don't make any permanent changes."

"Ben! That's great!" Jenna cried.

Peter joined in excitedly. "And they know we're going to build sets and everything? I mean, we can't promise that no one will spill paint or something by accident."

Ben smiled happily. "That's the beauty—they don't care! It's just a small warehouse with brick walls and a bare concrete floor. They store their excess inventory in it before they ship it on the train. And right now, it's completely empty."

"That's so perfect!" Leah said.

Then everyone else—almost everyone else— jumped in and started talking at once. In Nicole's disappointment over missing Jesse, she barely cared enough to listen, but the rest of the group was into it; that much was clear. Peter was already proposing extra meetings. Melanie thought they ought to get a notice in the newspaper. Jenna wanted committees.

I'm hungry, Nicole realized suddenly, and her stomach growled angrily.

She'd been lying when she'd told her mother she would eat at the meeting. At the time she'd had no intention of putting even an ounce of food into the stomach exposed by her model's midriff—not with Jesse there to see it. But now Jesse wasn't coming. . . .

And so who cares anymore? she thought, grabbing a paper plate and filling it with more macaroni salad then she'd eaten in a year. She pushed the salad to one side to make room for some chicken wings and a big helping of her mother's meatballs, then dropped into the nearest chair and began eating as if dying of hunger.

"I think we ought to stay open three nights," Peter was saying, in response to a question from Miguel. "Halloween's on a Saturday this year, so we could hold the haunted house on Thursday, Friday, and Saturday."

"Why not longer?" Ben asked. "I can get the key to the building tomorrow."

"Good," Peter said, "but this thing won't come together overnight. Halloween is only a week and a half away, and we'll be pushing to be ready by Wednesday. Can everyone work this weekend?"

An animated discussion ensued among the others while Nicole shoveled the last bite of macaroni into her mouth and began tearing through the meatballs. Everything tasted so good—as if she hadn't eaten in weeks.

You haven't, she told herself bitterly. First had come the summertime diet to look impressive for the new school year, then the renewed diet in September to try to get Jesse's attention. Most recently she'd practically starved herself to enter the U.S. Girls contest.

Yeah, good job, she thought, getting up to fill the empty spots on her plate with cheese and chips—two items she hadn't tasted in months because of their high fat content. *All that suffering really paid off. Leah won the stupid contest, and Jesse not only didn't come to your party, he didn't even call.*

"Is anyone ready for cake?" she asked, interrupting the meeting as she reached for a second plate.

"I'll have some," Ben called back immediately. "A big piece."

"Let's *all* have big pieces," she said, beginning to carve it up. She passed plates of cake around the room as the others attempted to make a plan.

"Okay," Jenna said, consulting her stenographer's pad. "Let's see. That's Leah and me on fliers, signs, banners, and tickets." She turned to Leah. "We can figure out how to split it up later."

Leah nodded and Jenna returned to her notes. "Ben's in charge of the building . . . getting the key and arranging things with ComAm. Peter'll talk to his father about publicity and see if we can get in the paper somehow."

Peter leaned forward. "I'll talk to the school drama department, too, to see what help they can give us, and I'll coordinate the volunteers— including the adults we get to chaperone."

Jenna scribbled all that down. "Good. Miguel, you're in charge of building the sets. Jesse will help you, and Melanie will paint them. That leaves you, Nicole. What do you want to do?"

"Huh?" Nicole looked up guiltily, her mouth crammed full of cake. "Oh, um, what's left?"

"Someone has to be in charge of costumes," Leah said. "That seems like a great job for you, Nicole. You can figure out what we should dress up as to scare people once they're inside, and you can help everyone get their costumes together."

"Yeah, okay. Whatever." With cake still in her mouth, Nicole bit into a chicken wing.

Everyone agreed to meet at the ComAm building to decorate on Saturday morning, and a few minutes later the meeting broke up. Nicole set down her plate with a couple of bites still on it as the others rose to their feet. All of a sudden, she wasn't feeling so hot.

"Do you have to leave already?" she asked plaintively. "We've still got plenty of food."

"I'm stuffed," said Leah, putting a hand to her flat stomach. Melanie nodded in agreement even though she'd only eaten a piece of cake.

"You should have told us you were having so much food, and I'd have skipped dinner," Miguel told her.

"It was great, though," Jenna added, flashing her a smile. "Thanks for going to so much trouble."

"Yeah. Thanks, Nicole," other voices echoed. And then they were gone. Nicole was left on her own with a basement full of leftovers.

"Great," she muttered, looking over the half-full chafing dishes, the battered remnant of cake, and the crumb-littered tablecloths. "All that work for nothing, and now I have to clean up, too." For a moment, she was almost angry with Jesse; then the emotion passed back into disappointment.

I'll have to get a plastic bag for that cut-up cheese and do something with the chips, she thought as she approached the tables. Not to mention all the washing up. Running a procrastinating finger through the icing left behind on the cake's waxed sheet of cardboard, Nicole popped the glob into her mouth. Instead of being sweet and delicious, though, as it had been the first time she'd tasted it, now it was greasy and gross. Nearly gagging, she spit the wad into a napkin and tossed the mess into the trash.

She felt awful—so bloated that her tight contest

jeans nearly cut her in half, and more than twice as depressed as she'd been before she'd eaten all that food. What could she have been thinking? Just because Jesse wasn't coming to her house that night didn't mean she had to make a total pig of herself. She still had to go to school the next day. She'd still see Jesse on Saturday.

"I feel like I'm going to throw up," she groaned, wishing it were true. At that moment, vomiting seemed like the best idea she'd ever had. With a sigh, she began fishing leftover sodas out of the ice water and lining them up on the table. When she had finished, she lifted the heavy tub and took it into the basement bathroom to empty into the shower.

"Oh, sick!" she gasped when she caught sight of her reflection in the mirror. She didn't just *feel* bloated, she *was* bloated. Her stomach stuck out noticeably, hard and round beneath the knot of her midriff top. She set the drink tub in the shower and straightened up for a better look.

I'm going to gain ten pounds, she thought, gazing into the mirror. *At least!* A wave of nausea washed over her. *I can't go to sleep with all this food in my stomach.*

She thought about staying up all night, or running around the block until she was exhausted, but then an easier way occurred to her. She was already half sick. It wouldn't take much. . . .

Raising the toilet seat, Nicole dropped to her knees in front of the bowl. She gathered her hair with one hand and leaned down close to the water, concentrating on how sick she felt. Her stomach rumbled. She gagged, but nothing else happened. She was so close. Holding her breath, she put a finger down her throat.

The contents of her stomach suddenly vaulted up out of her mouth. Nicole retched and retched, kicking the door shut behind her so no one would hear. It all came up . . . the chicken, the cake, the meatballs. The sight was so revolting that she puked all over again.

At last her nausea subsided. Rising on shaky legs, she flushed the toilet and washed her face in the sink. There was a tube of toothpaste in the medicine cabinet. She squeezed some onto a finger and ran it around her mouth, trying to kill that putrid taste. Then she stumbled back into the main room and opened a diet soda.

I had to do that, she told herself, shaken. She hadn't even known she knew how to induce vomiting— she'd certainly never done it before. That was something bulimics did. People with problems. Not her. She'd never been more disgusted. Just thinking about kneeling down in front of the toilet that way . . . on purpose . . . She wasn't sure she wasn't going to vomit again.

Nicole's hand trembled as she set her soda on

the table. *I had to do it this once,* she repeated. *If I'd gone to bed that full, I'd have gained ten pounds for sure. I'll never do it again, though, no matter how much I eat.*

She glanced toward the bathroom door and shuddered. "I promise," she whispered.

Five

"Thank God it's Friday!" Jenna said after school, climbing into the passenger side of Peter's blue Toyota. "What a week."

"It was kind of weird," Peter said, buckling his seat belt. "It was hard to keep my mind off what was going on with Jesse."

Jenna looked down at her Spirit Day outfit of forest green cords and a gold turtleneck sweater and nodded. "With everyone running around in school colors today, all I could think about was Jesse missing the game tonight, and how it must be killing him. Do you think he's going to help us with the haunted house tomorrow?"

Peter shrugged as he started the car. "I don't know. I got the impression Melanie was hiding something last night."

Jenna nodded. "Yeah. Me too. Do you think those two are . . . you know, together?" she asked hesitantly.

Peter turned his gaze from the road to smile at

her incredulously. "Jesse and Melanie? No. No way."

He seemed awfully sure of his answer. Jenna felt a twinge of . . . she wasn't sure what.

"Haven't you noticed the way they're always together at lunch?" she persisted. "And he drives her nearly everywhere. Maybe they're seeing each other in secret."

"I drive you nearly everywhere too," Peter said, "so it obviously doesn't mean much." There was a strange look in his eyes. A moment later, she found out why. "Besides, not *everybody* keeps who they like a secret."

"Oh, not again," Jenna groaned, putting her hands to her head. "Are you ever going to forgive me for that? I said I was sorry."

"What's there to forgive? Who you like is your business."

"Funny, that's what I thought," Jenna muttered. At least she *had*. Ever since Peter had found out about her futile crush on Miguel, he'd been holding it against her. She knew he was upset that she hadn't told him her secret, but it was just that the information had been so private . . . so personal. Anyway, it was definitely time for him to get over it.

"Isn't that behind us?" she asked. "I mean, Miguel is with Leah now and I'm completely over him."

"Really?" Peter looked at her again, his blue eyes sharp with interest. "You're over him?"

"Yeah. Well . . . mostly. It doesn't really matter, does it?"

"I guess not." Peter returned his attention to the road, his lips pressed into a line.

Great, Jenna thought. *Now he's sulking. Like I haven't suffered enough already!*

Every time she tried to picture herself at the upcoming homecoming dance, she could barely see herself there. What she saw instead was Miguel and Leah in each other's arms, having the time of their lives. Even in her imagination, it hurt.

Still, she'd decided she wanted to go. And she wanted Peter to take her. Jenna snuck a look at her friend's sullen profile, wondering if she ought to drop a few hints. Somehow, it didn't seem like the best possible time to bring it up.

Oh well, she thought with a sigh. The dance was still two weeks away, and they were going to be working on the haunted house together all day Saturday.

He'll probably ask me tomorrow, she thought. After all, who else would he ask?

"Here, let me do that, Mom," said Miguel, removing a cucumber from Mrs. del Rios's hand. "I hope I cook well enough to make a salad, at least. Why don't you sit down?"

"I'm really not that fragile, Miguel." But she slipped into one of the vinyl-upholstered metal chairs at their dinette just the same. He could tell she was tired, and he guessed that her feet hurt again. He took it out on the lettuce, whacking up the head with a big butcher's knife.

"You're supposed to *tear* the lettuce," Rosa informed him as she carried an armload of plates and silverware to the table.

"You do it your way and I'll do it mine," Miguel retorted, giving the pile one last wallop before sliding the finely chopped pieces off the cutting board into the salad bowl.

"How was school?" his mother asked as he turned his aggression toward the cucumber. "Did anything interesting happen?"

"No, it was awful," he replied without thinking. "Everyone's way too excited about Leah winning that modeling thing. It's already getting old."

"Who's Leah?"

Miguel's eyes flew open wide. What had he just said? The tomato paid the price as he tried to weasel out of it.

"Just a girl," he said, keeping his back to his mother. "She's in that group I'm earning the bus with."

"Oh. Is she nice?"

"She's all right." He felt like the worst kind of traitor as he added the tomato to the bowl, but what else could he say? That he loved her? That he dreamed about her day and night?

Yeah, that would go over huge, he thought, pouring half a bottle of dressing onto the vegetable hash he'd made of the salad. His anxiety about Leah's reaction to learning of his mother's illness was nothing compared to the actual fear he felt when he imagined his mother's reaction to Leah.

After all, his mother hadn't given up believing he'd come back to the Catholic Church. If she were to find out her only son was serious about a Jewish-Lutheran girl who didn't even know if she believed in God . . . well . . . *seven* kidneys probably wouldn't save her. Miguel shook his head at the thought. Ever since his father had died, his mother seemed to live for the dream of seeing her children in two huge church weddings, followed by the christenings and confirmations of many little grandchildren.

The worst thing was, Miguel wasn't sure he didn't want that too. Not the hoopla, so much. Not the church, per se. But that family—that community of people around him.

If he were ever to completely sever those ties, if he were to marry outside the church, it would break his mother's heart. And as much as he loved Leah, his family was everything to him now. The mere thought of disappointing his mother that way made him weak with worry.

Besides, this is all so ridiculous, he thought, carrying the salad to the table. *Leah and I are too young to even think about marriage, so there's no point involving our parents yet. Not for a good long time.* He nodded, convinced.

Now if only I could convince Leah.

This bites, Jesse thought miserably, huddling down into his leather jacket. It was freezing at the top of the Mapleton stands, but the cold was nothing compared to the sting of sitting out the game. *Look at Spenser out there, running around like he owns the field. That ought to be me!*

Even though getting caught would mean disaster, Jesse had slipped out his bedroom window and taken a bus to the Mapleton game, unable to sneak out his car with his father at home and equally unable to stay away. He couldn't stand the limbo he was in—half on the team and half off, not sure how the coach was leaning. Ironically, the stress of worrying about being cut made him want to drink more than ever.

He glanced quickly around him. At the top of the bleachers, where he was perched, the crowd was pretty thin. He had managed to get up there without seeing anyone he knew, and no one was watching him now. Working swiftly, he twisted the cap off the flask in his jacket and ducked his head to grab a swig from the hidden bottle. He knew he was nuts to be drinking there, of all places, but he couldn't help it. He was under too much pressure.

76

There was a sudden, enormous groan from the Mapleton crowd. Jesse lowered his flask to see Eric Spenser with another completion in his arms, streaking for the end zone. It looked as if the Wildcats were in for an easy win. Jesse raised the vodka to his lips again, knowing he should be happier about that than he was. After all, he still wanted to play in the state finals when he got back on the team.

If you get back on the team, he reminded himself, putting his flask away. Everything was so uncertain now. It seemed inconceivable that he might be kicked off the Wildcats for good, yet he knew how likely that was. Especially if he didn't shape up. He put his hand to his jacket, feeling the hard outline of the flask underneath. If anyone saw him drinking, he'd be finished with football for sure. He had to give it up, at least around people from school. It was way too risky not to.

It's kind of a moot point anyway, he thought, closing his eyes as Eric made another stellar run and the home crowd moaned its disappointment. After they'd returned from the principal's office when Jesse had been suspended, Dr. Jones had called a man to come out and install a lock on the liquor cabinet. Elsa had almost popped a vein at the sight of a regular, everyday workman drilling holes in her precious cabinetry, but his father had ignored all her pleas—for once. The lock had gone in. If it hadn't, Jesse knew he'd still be sneaking stuff from home.

Although it would be a lot trickier now, he admitted. Before, with both his "parents" drinking every night and no one paying attention, stealing liquor had been a cinch. He'd fill up a bottle an ounce at a time and no one had ever noticed. But all that remained of his old supply was now hidden in his jacket, and when it was gone he didn't know how he'd replace it. He couldn't exactly walk into a store and flash them a fake ID—not in a town as small as Clearwater Crossing. It might work for a while, but sooner or later he'd be recognized. No, he'd have to find someone to buy the stuff for him. And even then he ran the risk of something getting back to Coach Davis.

This bites, he thought again, huddling down into his jacket.

Melanie stood in line outside the Mapleton girls' bathroom, impatient for her turn. She'd shivered on the sidelines the entire game while the rest of the CCHS squad cheered. Now all she wanted was to use the facilities and catch a ride home in someone's nice, warm car.

"Hurry up," she muttered as the line inched slowly forward. "I'm freezing to death out here."

"No kidding," a voice behind her agreed. "At this rate, our friends'll graduate without us."

Melanie turned around. The girl who had spoken was a beauty, with auburn hair so dark it was almost brunette, flawless pale skin, and the kind of piercing green eyes a person would remember long after they'd forgotten the rest. She wore a red-and-white cheerleading jacket with the name *Amber* in fancy embroidery on the breast.

"Hey, you're on the Red River squad!" Melanie said, recognizing their rival school's colors. "What are you doing here?"

Amber smiled. "Just checking the competition. How about you? I saw you sitting on the bench."

"Yeah, well, that's a long story." Melanie didn't want to tell it, either. But then it occurred to her that Amber might have some interesting information. "You know that flip you guys do up onto the spirit pyramid?" she asked.

Amber shook her head. "Not really."

"Yeah, you know. You make a regular pyramid, except that the top girl takes a run at it from behind, jumps onto a trampoline, then flips in the air and lands on top? I was wondering where you all got the idea to do that. Did you learn it at camp or something?"

"I don't know who told you we do that!" Amber laughed, shaking her head. "I'm not even sure it's doable."

Huh? Melanie thought. "Oh, it's doable," she said slowly. "Are you sure you never—"

"No way," Amber said decisively. "Are you kidding? Our coach would never let us do something that dangerous. How could you spot it?" She shook her head again. "No way."

Melanie was shocked. How could CCHS's squad captain, Vanessa, have been so wrong about their competition? Not to mention wrong about the stunt itself? When Vanessa had proposed they do that flip, she'd acted as if it were totally routine, something that was done all the time.

Melanie's hand wandered unconsciously to the little patch of stubble on the back of her head. Apparently Vanessa wasn't as smart as she wanted them all to believe.

Six

"Mariana del Rios, here for her dialysis appointment," Miguel announced to the woman behind the counter in the medical-center lobby. Miguel knew his mother was perfectly capable of announcing herself, but doing it for her made him feel as if he were helping somehow. In reality, there was no need for an announcement at all. The staff was used to seeing his mother at seven every Saturday morning.

"Hello," the receptionist said cheerily. "Carol's running just a few minutes behind today, so if you'll all take a seat . . ."

Miguel tried to suppress his annoyance as he sat with his mother and Rosa in the standard doctor's office chairs. He hated it when the nurse who performed the procedure was late, but complaining about it upset his mother. He looked her over as she took a seat and folded her hands to wait. Her graying black hair was pulled smoothly into its normal neat bun, and a touch of makeup colored her cheeks, but he'd seen her look much better. A few short years ago, she'd been as beautiful as his sister.

"Mom, can I take some canned food to school on Monday?" Rosa asked as they waited. "We're having a food drive to help the poor."

Miguel flinched involuntarily. *The poor? What are we?* he wondered.

His mother didn't seem to share his sense of irony. "Of course, *mi hija*," she replied. "Take two cans of soup from the cupboard."

Rosa smiled, satisfied.

Miguel opened his mouth to protest, then abruptly shut it again. It was ridiculous to be helping "the poor" when they were on public assistance themselves. On the other hand, a couple cans of soup weren't going to matter either way. Besides, he knew what would happen if he complained. His mother would tell him the story of the widow's mites—again.

He already knew it by heart. One day Jesus and his disciples were hanging out at the temple watching everyone give their offerings to the treasury. Some people put in a lot of money, but when a poor widow showed up, she put in only two little coins—mites—worth practically nothing. Then Jesus said something like, "That woman gave more than all the others. They had a lot to give and they have a lot left over, but she's given all that she had."

A couple of coins, a couple of cans of Campbell's, Miguel thought. *Whatever.* It wasn't as if he were *opposed* to helping people out. And as soon as he graduated from high school, he was going to get a job—a *good* job that would pay all their bills with a little left over. The del Rios family wouldn't be on public assistance forever. Miguel tried to imagine his father's reaction if he could see how far they'd fallen without him. Living in public housing now, dependent on Medicaid . . .

"So, what are you doing after this?" his mother asked, breaking into his thoughts. "Any particular plans?"

He nodded. "Eight Prime is putting together a haunted-house fund-raiser for next weekend. I'm supposed to help set it up, so I'll probably be there all day."

"You should have told me!" Mrs. del Rios cried. "You didn't have to drive me, Miguel. I could have gotten a ride with someone else, like I do the rest of the week. Please don't plan your Saturdays around me, *mi vida.* You should have some fun now and then, while you can."

Miguel's jaw tightened. The only thing that bothered him more than his mother relying on other people to take her to midweek dialysis appointments was when they bailed out on her and she had to take the bus. Mrs. del Rios had never learned to drive and she wasn't interested in starting now—especially when they could only afford one car. Even so, she was always trying to get rid of him or telling him to do things with his friends. The week before, she had sent him and Rosa off to the grocery store once she'd been hooked up to the machine, but Miguel had come back the moment he'd unloaded the food.

"I've already told you that as long as I'm the man of this family, I'll never miss one of your Saturday appointments," he said, settling stubbornly into his chair.

He took a deep breath and managed a smile. "Never," he repeated. "I promise."

"Oh man, my head," Jesse groaned. "I should have done this later." As he pushed the roaring gas mower over the Joneses' huge front lawn, every sound it made, every jolt and vibration, went through his temples like a hot, thin blade. He held stubbornly to the handles, determined to finish in spite of the hangover that made his brain feel too large for his skull.

You ought to enjoy this hangover, he thought sarcastically. *Savor it. It could be your last for a while.* He'd ended up drinking the entire contents of his jacket flask—the last of his easy liquor supply—at the game the night before.

A movement down on the street caught his eye as he turned at the edge of the yard. A blue Toyota was pulling up to the curb. A moment later, Peter Altmann got out and headed toward him.

Great. Jesse grimaced as Peter made his way across the half-mowed grass. *Isn't it bad enough that I'm already depressed and hungover? The last thing I need now is a confrontation with holier-than-thou, minors-shouldn't-drink Altmann.* Jesse still remembered his last conversation with Nicole, when she'd been dumb enough to tell him that Peter and Jenna were critical of his drinking. *He's probably mad at me for missing the Thursday meeting.* Jesse killed the motor on the mower and braced himself for a lecture.

"Hi! You're up early," Peter said as he closed the final few feet between them. "How's it going?"

Peter's smile was friendly, his posture relaxed. He didn't *look* like someone about to go off on a tirade.

"All right," Jesse ventured cautiously.

"I just wanted to make sure you got the word about the haunted house. Ben's dad came through with a building for us, and we're all going over there now to get it ready. Want me to give you a lift?"

Jesse shook his head. "Can't," he said gruffly. "I have to finish the lawn."

Peter nodded. "Why not let me help you? It'll be faster with two people, and then we can both go together." He reached to take the mower handle, but Jesse jerked it back.

"It's a one-person job." His voice came out harder than he had intended, especially since Peter had apparently decided to spare him the sermon. "I mean, thanks anyway, but it's under control."

"Well, I could always rake up the cuttings. Have you got any bags? Or what do you usually—"

"Peter, I don't need any help. You'd better go on without me or you're going to be late."

Peter hesitated. "Okay," he said at last. "But let me give you the address so you'll be able to find us when you finish here. I'll just go get some paper from the car." He turned and began walking in that direction.

Jesse sighed. Peter wasn't getting it. "Look, don't bother," he called out. "I'm quitting Eight Prime. Melanie should have told you."

Peter turned slowly back around. "As a matter of fact, she did," he admitted. "This morning. I just didn't want to believe it."

"Well, believe it," Jesse said. "You guys are the Magnificent Seven now . . . Seven Prime. Oh wait—seven is already a prime number. Look, I don't know, just leave me out of it."

"But you said you'd stick with us until we earned a bus for the kids. I can't believe you're going back on your word."

Jesse's head was throbbing. "I know what I said. But it isn't working out, okay? I'm sorry I ever made you that promise."

"Me?" Peter shook his head. "Forget what you

promised me, all right? What about what you promised Jason? That kid believes in you."

"Yeah, well, that's part of the problem. I'm not exactly a role model for the Junior Explorers now, am I? It's better if Jason forgets me."

"Better for who?" Peter challenged. "You made that kid a promise, and what's worse, you made him like you. How do you think he's going to feel if you abandon him now?"

"Peter—"

"Look, Jesse, I know you've had a lousy week, but let's be honest with each other. You've been drinking all along, right? I mean, I doubt you just started the night you got caught. And you didn't think you were a bad role model before. The only difference is that now everyone knows you got in trouble, and you're embarrassed by it."

"Wouldn't you be?" Jesse demanded.

There was a trace of a smile on Peter's face again. "To say the least. But listen: a person who makes a mistake, regrets it, and turns his life around is a fine example for kids. A quitter, on the other hand . . . well, that's the worst example there is."

Jesse shrugged. He could see Peter's point. He just didn't want to admit it.

"Jesse, please. Don't make me tell those kids you're giving up on them. Come with me this morning and help."

Jesse scuffed a foot in the grass, torn between keeping his promise and running from his problems. He could barely imagine facing Eight Prime. On the other hand, on Monday he would have to face the entire school. It would be nice to be sure of a few friends, at least.

"I couldn't go even if I wanted to," he admitted at last. "I'm grounded. Until Monday."

Peter nodded thoughtfully. "I guess you have to respect your parents' decision, but can't you at least *ask* your dad? Maybe he'll let you help after all, since it's for charity."

"No way," Jesse said firmly. Asking would mean he'd actually have to talk to the man.

"But if you tell him that people are counting on you . . . We hardly have any time to pull this together, Jesse. Hey, I know! Tell him you'll make up for today by being grounded *two* extra days next week."

"Gee, that sounds fun."

"Jesse—"

"All right, all right, I'll ask him," Jesse said, letting go of the lawnmower and moving reluctantly toward his front door. "But there's no way he's going for this."

"You never know," Peter said. He pulled the starter cord and the mower roared to life again, ending the conversation. He waved before he pushed it expertly across the lawn.

You've got to hand it to the guy, Jesse thought as he walked off in search of his father. *No wonder he can't stand quitters.*

"Jesse! Hey, Jesse!" Jason's excited voice rang out at the front of the storehouse.

Nicole was working with a pile of costumes, but she spun around in time to see Peter and Jesse pull up at the curb and Jason take off like a shot, headed for his hero. A few feet short of launching himself into Jesse's arms, the little towhead seemed to remember his dignity and skidded to a stop, totally off balance.

Just like me, Nicole thought ironically, hurriedly turning her back on the scene. *But in a different kind of way.* Despite her calm exterior, her heart was pounding excitedly, and she could barely think about anything except how happy she was to see him. *I wonder why he's riding with Peter?*

It was hard to imagine Jesse preferring Peter's road-weary Tercel to his own flashy car. For that matter, it was strange that Peter hadn't come early to mind the Junior Explorers. His college-age partner, Chris Hobart, Chris's girlfriend, Maura, and a few of their college friends had shown up to see the kids safely dropped off. Nicole considered this a moment longer, then dismissed the question of Peter and Jesse's strange new togetherness with a shrug. *He's here. Who cares how he got here?*

"How's it going, Nicole?" asked Leah, appearing at her side. "What a circus, huh?" She put her hands on her hips and looked around. Nicole straightened up and did likewise.

They were just outside the main door of the storehouse. Inside, the sounds of Miguel, Chris, and the other college guys hammering and sawing were nearly deafening. Melanie was somewhere inside too, trying to paint sets that weren't even built yet, and Jenna and her sister Caitlin were setting up a ticket-taking arrangement near the entry. Ben was running around "supervising" in shorts and black hightops, an absurdly enormous key ring through his front belt loop giving him the appearance of a cartoon prison warden. And, if that weren't enough chaos, the Junior Explorers were there to "help."

Right, Nicole thought, shaking her head. Danny and Priscilla were already fighting, Cheryl was crying because Lisa said her dress was ugly, and Amy was clinging to Melanie like a two-armed octopus. *They're tons of help*.

"Could you use a hand with these costumes?" Leah asked. "I'm not doing anything right now."

"That would be great!" Nicole said. "I don't know why you all expect me to figure out what everyone else has to dress up as."

"Someone has to be in charge," Leah said. "Otherwise we could end up with things that don't fit our theme, or people dressed up the same way. What have you got so far?"

Nicole rolled her eyes. "A pile of junk is what it looks like. Peter got Ms. Kazinski to loan us all this stuff from the drama club, but I have to keep track of it and make sure it's returned. I don't even know what all's in here." She poked gingerly at the heap of clothes, as if something alive might be lurking just beneath the surface.

"You'd better make a list before you pass anything out, then." Leah took a pen from her back pocket and looked around for something to write on. Nicole handed her a pad. "You hold up the clothes, and I'll make an inventory," Leah said.

"Okay." Nicole lifted the item on top. "This is the best thing I've found so far. It's a cloak, I think, but it'll make a good Dracula cape."

"Oh, definitely," Leah agreed. "Who's going to be Dracula?"

"I haven't decided yet," Nicole lied. Jesse would be Dracula. Obviously.

"What else do you have?" Leah asked.

There was another, less elaborate cape, followed by a black shawl, then a rust-colored one.

"Who wears shawls?" Nicole complained.

"Actors, I guess. We'll think of some way to use them. What else?"

Nicole held up an ornate period gown of

tarnished gold satin and ivory lace. "I have *no* idea what to do with this. It's pretty, but we're putting on a haunted house, not *Hamlet*."

"I'll wear it," Leah offered instantly.

Nicole looked suspiciously from Leah back to the dress, wondering if she was missing something. "It's not exactly scary."

"I'll make it scary—trust me. Besides, that's one costume done you can cross off your list." Leah fished a rectangular ivory lace shawl from the pile. "*And* one less shawl to deal with."

"Suit yourself," Nicole said with a shrug.

In a few minutes they had sorted the pile. There was a long black dress that Nicole had immediately grabbed for herself. But now she hesitated. Should she take the other black cape and be a vampire, like Jesse? Or would that be too obvious? And would a female vampire even wear a cape? She chewed her lip, trying to decide.

"I'm going to go put this dress in the car," Leah announced, dropping Nicole's pad and picking up her costume. "Back in a minute."

Nicole felt an anxious twinge as she watched Leah walk away. *Leah likes that dress so much, I probably should have worn it.* After all, Leah was a model now. She knew about these things.

Nicole picked up her own black dress and looked it over critically. A few weeks ago, she would have said she was much better at picking out clothes than Leah. Now even that minor confidence was shattered. Everyone at school thought Leah was so cool since she'd become a U.S. Girl. People were already starting to imitate her. And if Leah liked the other dress . . .

No, this one is good, Nicole reassured herself. *This one is better. Leah only took the other one to make things easy on you.*

She set the dress back down, hoping she was right. Then she picked up the good black cloak, a pair of black tuxedo pants, and a man's white dress shirt and looked around for Jesse.

He and Jason were down by the street, picking up trash and sweeping the sidewalk. It was the perfect chance to talk to him alone, and handing him his costume gave her the perfect excuse. Quickly, before Leah came back, Nicole walked down to meet him.

"Hi!" she said brightly—too brightly. Inside she groaned with frustration. Would she ever learn to stop doing that? "I, uh, brought you your costume. Do you want me to put it in Peter's car?"

Jesse stopped sweeping and leaned on his broom. "I guess. What is it?"

"You're going to be Dracula. I picked you out all the best stuff."

"I don't doubt it."

What was that supposed to mean? "Yeah, well," she said nervously, "I'll have to get you some fangs and makeup, but these are the clothes."

Jesse nodded. They stood there looking at each other, Nicole racking her brain for something intelligent to say.

"I guess you're pretty bummed about missing the Mapleton game last night," she finally ventured. "It's just so unfair that they didn't let you play! It's not—not—"

Nicole stammered uncertainly to a stop. Jesse was drawing his right hand across his throat, gesturing frantically for her to be quiet.

"Not here!" he whispered, nodding toward Jason a few feet away.

"Not here, what? I was only going to say I'm sorry you got suspended and—"

"For Pete's sake, Nicole, shut *up*!" he hissed. "I don't want Jason to know about that."

Nicole drew back a step, wounded. Jason was only a kid. What difference did it make what he knew?

"Fine. Excuse me for caring," she retorted angrily.

Jesse barely dropped his broom in time to catch the armload of clothes she flung at his face.

Seven

"That looks good to me," Jenna declared, straightening up and wiping her dirty hands on a rag. "What do you think?" she asked her sister.

Caitlin shrugged noncommittally. "Fine."

Jenna suppressed the rush of impatience she felt. She had invited Caitlin to come to the storehouse because she'd hoped that being around other people might help coax her sister out of her shell. Chris and Maura were there with college friends, for example, but instead of meeting them, Caitlin had stuck to Jenna all day, barely even speaking unless someone asked her a question. As frustrating as it was, though, Jenna was determined to stay nice.

"So where are the tickets?" Caitlin asked, pointing to Nicole's old card table. It had been pressed into service again, this time draped with some dark-colored shawls Nicole had found in the costume stuff.

"What? Oh. Leah's making those on her computer at home. But when we get them, we'll put them in here." Jenna pressed her palm down into an empty shoe box she'd covered with pumpkin-embellished gift wrap. "Then, when we sell a ticket, we'll put the money in here." She patted the old cash box, the lid of which she'd also papered. "People will line up over there," she continued, pointing. "When we take their tickets, we'll put them in the other shoe box."

Jenna walked between a couple of old ropes the girls had rigged waist high, pretending she was moving through the line. At the end of the ropes was an old crate Melanie had spray-painted black, topped by a black shoe box with a slot cut in the lid. She pretended to drop a ticket inside it.

"I still don't know why you don't just tear the used tickets in half and throw them away," Caitlin said.

"I could," Jenna admitted. "But it will be fun to count them later and see how many people came."

"You could always count the money instead."

"I know, but it won't be as accurate. All the Junior Explorers are getting in for free, and so are their friends and families. And if I know Peter, he'll give other kids free tickets, too. On the other hand, some people will probably pay more than they have to, just to help us out. The only way to be sure how many people come through is to take a ticket from everyone and count them up at the end."

Caitlin's only reply was a shrug.

Working with Cat is about as exciting as breathing, Jenna thought, looking longingly for Peter. She spotted him at the other end of the building, rolling a coat of black paint onto a makeshift wall while Melanie added details to a wall that had already dried.

Peter had called Jenna early that morning to tell her he wanted to stop by Jesse's and to see if she could get another ride. She'd expected that once he got there, he'd help her and Caitlin design their ticket-taking arrangement, but things hadn't worked out that way. Peter had barely set foot through the storehouse door when Melanie had commandeered him.

"Peter!" she'd cried. "Could you give me a hand?" And Peter had run off to help her.

Granted, Melanie had several buckets of paint, a bunch of spray cans, brushes, rollers, drop cloths, and a big wooden ladder to drag around. She obviously needed Peter's help more than Jenna and Caitlin did. But it was still annoying the way those two had spent all morning working together, with barely a word for anyone else.

Barely a word for you, you mean. Jenna had been telling herself for hours not to be such a baby, that everyone had to pitch in together to get the haunted house ready in time. Still, it was impossible not to notice how close her best friend and

CCHS's most wanted were getting. Peter hung on every word Melanie said, and Melanie had been teasing and laughing all day.

As Jenna watched, Peter said something that sent Melanie into giggles again. Her laughter rang through the storehouse, almost as if she *wanted* people to hear. She dipped her brush into a bucket of gory red paint and pretended to flick it at Peter. Peter played along, raising his arms in mock horror, smiling the whole time.

Jenna turned her back on the scene abruptly and grabbed a plastic bag full of cotton spiderwebs. "So, what's next?" she asked Caitlin. "I think we ought to put up these spiderwebs."

Caitlin looked uncertain. "Shouldn't we ask Melanie to paint these walls black first?"

"No!" Jenna said, with a bit too much emphasis. "I mean, we're not allowed to paint any permanent walls. Besides, it's going to be dark, and the brick's kind of cool."

Another cascade of giggles sounded from the far end of the building. Jenna ripped the spiderweb bag open with so much force that the contents spewed out and landed on Caitlin's feet.

"All right, so I'll hang spiderwebs," Caitlin muttered, picking them up. "Don't get so excited."

"Can I help you?" Melanie asked. She had stepped out of the storehouse in search of a trash

98

can and had found a tall blond woman with a camera around her neck standing on the pavement.

"Yes. Hi," the stranger said, glancing down at a long, narrow steno pad she held in her right hand. "I'm looking for Peter Altmann. Is he here?"

"Who are you?" Melanie countered.

"Susan Graham." The woman switched the pad to her left hand and extended her right to shake. "I'm with *The Clearwater Herald*. I spoke to Peter's father on the phone, and he said—"

"Oh! Yeah, right," Melanie interrupted excitedly, dropping the paper drop cloth she'd been taking to the trash and hurriedly putting a rock on top to keep it from blowing away. "Come on in."

"Wow! This is quite an undertaking," Susan said as she and Melanie wove through the chaos of construction inside the building. "I thought there were only eight of you."

"What? Oh. You mean in Eight Prime." Melanie gestured around with one arm. "There are a lot of volunteers here today, too. We have a bunch of students from Clearwater University because Peter's partner in the Junior Explorers, Chris Hobart, goes there and he brought them. Then there are the Junior Explorers, of course." Melanie stepped over a pile of wood scraps someone had left on the floor, motioning for Susan to follow. "Plus I think there are a couple of people from the CCHS drama club here. I don't know—you'll have to ask Peter." She had to shout the last sentence to be heard over the sudden whine of a nearby electric saw.

"Where did all this wood come from?" Susan shouted back.

"Peter got it donated by a place that recycles building materials. It's all scrap from things they've torn down around town. I guess they sell what they can and give away stuff that's too beat-up to sell." Melanie smiled and shrugged her shoulders. "What do we care? We're painting everything black anyway."

Susan smiled back. "I can see that," she said, making a note on her pad.

"Look, there's Peter." They had reached the end of the storehouse. "Hey, Peter!" Melanie called. "Come down a minute."

Peter twisted around on the ladder, a roller dripping black paint in one hand. "Hi," he said. He hurried down and extended his hand to Susan, then quickly pulled it back again. "Oops, sorry. I just about covered you with paint."

Melanie felt her heart pull at the sight of the smile he flashed Susan in place of a handshake. It had amazed her before the way Peter could smile that way for total strangers, as if he were truly excited to meet them. It was just so . . . good.

"Hi, Peter. I'm Susan Graham with *The Clearwater Herald*. Your father called me about your haunted house and said you'd love to get a mention in the paper."

"We sure would!" Peter put down the roller, grabbed an old towel off the floor, and hurriedly wiped his hands. "Wow, thanks for coming! Did my dad explain why we're raising money?"

"Briefly. I'd like to get the story from you, though." Susan held her pen over her pad expectantly.

Peter nodded. "Well, let's see. I guess it all starts with Kurt Englbehrt."

"Kurt Englbehrt?" Susan interrupted. "Isn't he the student who beat leukemia, then got killed in a car crash last month?"

"That's right. Eight of us met each other volunteering at that fund-raising carnival for Kurt. Then, when he was killed, we couldn't let it end that way. We wanted to do something to show we still cared. So we ended up calling ourselves Eight Prime, and we all agreed to stay together until we earned a bus for the Junior Explorers."

"Wait. Back up," said Susan, writing furiously. "What does Kurt have to do with the Junior Explorers?"

"Nothing, really. It's just that Kurt inspired us to do something good in his memory, and the Junior Explorers need a bus. It seemed fitting."

"Peter started the Junior Explorers all by himself," Melanie couldn't resist putting in. "Clearwater

Crossing Park let him start it and run it and everything, and he's only sixteen."

Susan's eyebrows shot up as she looked at Peter for confirmation.

Peter laughed. "Not all by myself," he corrected. "I doubt they would have given a fourteen-year-old his own program, no matter how good his intentions. I have a partner, Chris Hobart. Chris is twenty now."

"Right. Your friend here . . ." Susan turned to Melanie.

"Melanie Andrews," Melanie supplied, embarrassed by the sudden realization that she'd never introduced herself.

"Melanie," Susan continued, "mentioned Chris's name."

"Do you want to meet him?" Peter asked.

"Maybe later. If I understand correctly, it's Eight Prime that's putting on the haunted house. The Junior Explorers are the beneficiaries, not the principals."

"Uh, yeah," Peter said uncertainly. "I guess that's right."

"So who all's in Eight Prime?"

"That's easy," Melanie cut in again. "Me and Peter, Jenna Conrad, Leah Rosenthal, Ben Pipkin, Miguel del Rios, Jesse Jones, and Nicole Brewster." She tried to point to people as she named them, but so many partial walls had already been erected that she could no longer see all the way through the warehouse. Most of the members were out of sight. "I could go call them all together if you want," she volunteered.

"That would be perfect," Susan said. "I'd like to take everyone's picture outside somewhere—maybe on that little knoll next to the building. And while you're rounding everyone up, I'll ask Peter a few more questions."

Melanie nodded and began to hurry away.

"Get the Junior Explorers, too!" Peter shouted after her. "It'll give 'em the thrill of their lives to have their pictures in the paper."

Melanie found Ben first. He was attempting to help a couple of Chris's friends build one of the free-standing walls being used to divide the empty storehouse into makeshift rooms.

"Don't you have any better nails?" he complained to them as she walked up. "These are so flimsy they bend when I hammer them."

"That's because you have to hit them *straight*," one of the guys replied through clenched teeth. "The way you're whacking them sideways would bend a railroad spike."

"I think I know what I'm doing," Ben retorted. He picked a fresh nail out of the box, held it in position, and gingerly tapped it with a hammer.

Carefully he removed his bracing hand. Then he sidearmed the nail so hard that it bent all the way to the wood. "See?" he demanded. "There's something wrong with them!"

"Hey, Ben!" Melanie called hurriedly. The way the other two guys were glaring at him gave her the impression she'd arrived just in time. "Someone from the newspaper is here, and she wants to see Eight Prime outside."

Ben looked up. "This isn't a good time, Melanie," he said, frowning. "I'm trying to—"

"Are you kidding?" one of Chris's friends interrupted. "It's the press, man! You've got to go. Don't worry about us—we'll manage."

Ben reluctantly allowed his hammer to be pulled from his grasping fingers. "Well, if you really think you can do this without me . . ."

"They said they could. Come on, Ben." Melanie tugged at his shirt to hurry him along, then pointed him toward the door. She only lagged behind long enough to whisper to the guys Ben had been helping, "He's really not that weird, once you get to know him."

"I'd rather get to know *you*," one of them said behind her as she hurried off.

Melanie hesitated, then decided to ignore the comment. It would have been fun to flirt for a while, get them to ask her out, then watch them panic when they learned she was only fifteen. But she didn't have time right then.

"Hey, Miguel!" she shouted, spotting him on another construction crew.

A few minutes later, she'd found everyone but Jenna and had gathered her friends outside the main door. "I wonder where Jenna is?" she said.

"She's helping Maura out back with the Junior Explorers," Leah told her. The kids had been running around everywhere earlier in the day, but once construction had started in earnest, it hadn't seemed safe to have them in the warehouse. Maura and a friend had volunteered to take them to a grassy lot behind the building to play, and apparently Jenna had joined them later. "Do you want me to go get her?" Leah added.

"No, I'll go," Melanie said quickly, eager to be the one to tell Amy she was going to be in the newspaper. She imagined the little girl's eyes lighting up at the thrilling news. "I'll be right back."

The truth was she felt a little guilty for ignoring her young friend so long. Normally she and Amy were inseparable, but today Melanie hadn't minded a bit when Maura had herded up the kids and taken them outside.

I was having so much fun with Peter, in fact, I barely even noticed. The thought stopped her in her tracks.

Had Melanie Andrews, the self-appointed queen of misery, just admitted to having *fun*?

"I don't know about you, but I'm exhausted," Leah told Miguel as they carried armloads of wood scraps to the Dumpster out back. The chill fall sky was rapidly growing dark, and only Eight Prime remained at the warehouse.

"It's all this getting your picture taken," Miguel teased. He tossed his scraps into the big metal bin, then held the lid open for Leah. "How many modeling jobs does that make so far this month?"

"Getting my picture taken for the newspaper was *not* modeling," Leah protested hotly. She hated it when Miguel teased her about being a U.S. Girl. "Or if it was, then you're all models too now."

Miguel laughed as they headed back toward the entrance.

"So, what are you doing tomorrow?" Leah asked before they rejoined the others. "Want to get together?"

Miguel had shown up late that morning, as usual, but Leah knew from the time she'd spied on him that he was busy on Saturdays with chores like grocery shopping and mowing the lawn. Sunday was the day he was free.

"Sure," he said eagerly. "How about I pick you up in the morning and we hike around the lake? All the leaves are turning colors up there."

"No, not the lake," Leah groaned. "We *always* go to the lake."

Miguel seemed taken aback. "Well, what do you want to do?"

I want to go to your house! Leah almost shouted. *I want to meet your mother, and I want to be part of your life!* She took a deep breath and slowly counted to five.

"Why don't I come to your house?" she asked casually. "We could hang out and relax."

"No. Uh, that's not such a good idea. It's, um, going to be Sunday, and my mom and Rosa will be at mass half the day. At least."

"I don't mind."

"Well, she will. I told you my mom's old-fashioned. She'd have a fit if she knew I had a girl alone in the house with me."

"But we're alone together all the time!"

"Not in my bedroom."

"Who said we have to go in your bedroom? We could stay in the living room or—"

"Leah, just . . . what's the point? There's nothing to do at my house."

"You still haven't told her about me, have you?" Leah accused angrily. They were standing outside the front door now. "Your mom doesn't know I exist."

"Look, can we talk about this later? I really don't want the whole world to know our business."

"You don't want them to know we *have* business!

107

Why are you keeping us a secret, Miguel? Are you that ashamed of me?"

"Me?" Miguel protested. "You didn't want to tell anyone either. You thought it would make everyone in Eight Prime feel weird if they knew we were a couple, remember?"

"That was then!" Leah almost exploded. "Do you think they haven't guessed by now that something's going on? Melanie caught us that day in the library, and the rest of them see us together everywhere. Use your head, Miguel! They must know we're hiding something, and I think it's time we tell them."

Miguel scuffed a foot against the pavement, his eyes on his shoes. "I want to tell them too. But I thought maybe we could do it at the homecoming dance. I thought—"

"You thought that if we showed up as each other's dates and danced a few slow dances together we wouldn't actually have to *tell* anyone," Leah finished for him, certain she was right.

Miguel shrugged, his eyes still on the ground. "So you don't want to go to the dance with me, then?"

"Of *course* I want to go, but why can't—"

"There you guys are!" Peter interrupted, pushing the front door open. "We thought you got lost." He stepped out onto the pavement, the rest of the group crowding out behind him. "We're going to call it a night, all right? Ben's locking up."

"Uh, sure," Leah said uneasily, hoping no one had overheard her and Miguel arguing. She wanted Eight Prime to know they were a couple, but a big fight wasn't the way she wanted them to find out.

Everyone started wandering down to the street and their rides. "Don't forget!" Peter called after them. "Ask your parents if at least one of them can chaperone on at least one night. We'll get adult volunteers from church, but it's good to have as much help as we can."

"My mom couldn't possibly spend four hours here, standing outside in the cold," Miguel grumbled to Leah as he unlocked his car doors and let them in. "I'm not even going to ask her."

Oh, but it's okay for everyone else's parents, Leah thought angrily, buckling her seat belt. *And total strangers from Peter's church—they can freeze their butts off too. No problem.*

She stared out the window as Miguel started the car and began to drive, too upset even to speak to him. Not asking his mother to chaperone was just more of his evasion. Leah was sure of it. For whatever reason, he was determined to keep her from meeting his mom.

I ought to just show up over there tomorrow morning. Early, before Mrs. del Rios and Rosa go to church. For a moment, she seriously considered doing it.

Then she remembered. She wasn't even supposed

to know where Miguel lived. There was no way she could show up without admitting that she'd secretly followed him home one day.

Leah grimaced at the familiar rush of guilt triggered by the remembrance of that betrayal of his trust. *You ought to tell him what you did*, she thought for the millionth time. *Tell him, and tell him you're sorry.*

A moment later, though, she shook her head. There was enough tension in the relationship already without dropping a bomb like that one.

No, she decided. *I just need to make him invite me over. Once I officially know he lives in public housing, there won't be anything left to hide.*

Eight

The members of Eight Prime: (from left) Conrad, Pipkin, del Rios, Rosenthal, Altmann, Andrews, Jones, Brewster.

Haunted House Aids Worthy Cause
Local Teens Remember Classmate

By Susan Graham
Staff Writer

CLEARWATER CROSSING—This Halloween, when many will be thinking only of candy and parties, eight former classmates of deceased Clearwater Crossing High School student Kurt Englbehrt will be working to make a difference. Peter Altmann, Melanie

Andrews, Jenna Conrad, Leah Rosenthal, Ben Pipkin, Miguel de Rios, Jesse Jones, and Nicole Brewster—calling themselves Eight Prime—have dedicated themselves to the task of raising funds to buy a bus for an underprivileged children's group known as the Junior Explorers and donating the vehicle in Kurt's memory. It is a staggering undertaking for eight unassisted teens, yet taking on the seemingly impossible is nothing new for group leader Altmann.

"I saw the Junior Explorers as a way to make a difference, to help people out," said Altmann. "It was a way to show love for my neighbor, too, which is something I really believe in."

Altmann, 16, along with Chris Hobart, 20, founded the Junior Explorers two years ago. The program serves children from poor and broken homes by involving them in a wide range of fun, free activities each Saturday and for two weeks during the summer, when the Junior Explorers will ride their bus to a much-anticipated camp.

In order to make sure the kids have that bus in time, Eight Prime has already undertaken several fund-raising activities, the latest being the construction of an elaborate haunted house in the trackside ComAm storehouse.

"The ancient bus we started out with gave up the ghost last summer," quipped Hobart, gesturing to the spooky scenery being built all around him. "The city council promised us a new one, but then there was some kind of budget problem and our funding got cut. With any luck, this haunted house will bring us a big step closer to buying that bus on our own."

"I hope a lot of people will come out to support this," Andrews said. "Especially all the people who knew Kurt."

"Kurt had a lot of friends," Conrad added. "He's definitely missed. We know a bus won't bring him back, but it might make people feel a little better to know how much good it's doing."

If you want to help Eight Prime and the Junior Explorers, or if you're simply looking for a spook-tacular good time, stop by 153 Oak Street this Thursday, Friday, or Saturday night, from 7 to 11 P.M. Admission is $5 per person, children and adults.

It was right there on the first page of the Local Happenings section. Melanie smiled as she studied the picture, oblivious to the cold morning air that rushed through the open front door and swirled around her ankles. Susan had promised that she'd do her best to get an announcement in somewhere, but she'd refused to commit herself beyond that.

"It's all up to my editor," she'd said. "He'll decide how much room to give this and whether or not we print a picture. Or, for that matter, whether it'll go in at all."

It hadn't sounded very encouraging, but here was a major article in crisp, fresh black and white. The only teeny-tiny bummer was that the *Herald* had used a picture of Eight Prime alone, without the Junior Explorers. Melanie was afraid the kids would be disappointed, but Susan had warned that there might be a legal reason not to show the Junior Explorers' faces, and apparently the paper had decided not to risk it. Still, it was a good article, and right in the front of the section. *This ought to bring a lot of people out to the haunted house*, Melanie thought excitedly.

"Hey, Dad!" she shouted, pushing the front door shut distractedly and heading toward the kitchen. "Hey, Dad, look. I'm in the paper!"

Mr. Andrews was sitting at the breakfast bar, hunched over a cup of coffee. He straightened up slightly when she slid the paper in front of him.

"That's great, Mel," he said, his eyes skimming down the lines. "Congratulations. It sounds like quite an event." Despite that fact that he was obviously nursing a hangover, he seemed genuinely interested.

"It will be," Melanie said. "And now that it's been in the news, I'm sure a lot of people will come."

Then she remembered what Peter had said about everyone asking their parents to chaperone. She hadn't been sure that was such a good idea before, but her dad *had* been drinking less since her accident. And he did seem pretty into it—he was still looking at the article.

"What's this garbage Peter's spouting about loving his neighbor?" Mr. Andrews asked, pointing. "He sounds like a do-gooding Christian or something."

All the warm feelings Melanie had had a moment before disappeared like smoke. "Well . . . yeah. I thought you knew."

Her father looked up from the paper. "Now how was I supposed to know something like that? I thought he had more sense, actually."

So much for asking her father to chaperone at the haunted house. She'd never be able to see him and Peter in the same building again without worrying what he might say. Not to mention that most of the other adults there would be from Peter's church.

What was I even thinking? she wondered, wandering from the room.

"Well, I guess we're ready," Mrs. del Rios said. She was standing by the front door, putting on her hat. Rosa was beside her, dressed and ready for church.

"All right. See you later." Miguel leaned back into the sofa, eager for them to be gone. Ever since he'd stopped attending mass, this had become a moment he dreaded. Knowing his mom wanted him to go with them . . . not going. She never said anything, never made him feel pressured. But he knew he was letting her down, and that was bad enough.

"If you want to come with us, we'd love to have you," his mother said unexpectedly. "We could wait, if you want to change clothes."

Miguel froze. He hadn't set foot in church since his father's funeral, and she knew he didn't plan to. So why was she inviting him now, for no apparent reason?

His heart beat faster and the air in the room seemed suddenly stale. Was there something she wasn't telling him? Was she sicker than he knew? Maybe she wanted him along because in her heart she suspected there wouldn't be many more masses. The thought filled him with panic. For a moment, he seriously considered putting on his suit coat.

Then he shook his head. If his mom still wanted to worship God after everything God had done to them, he guessed that was her business.

Miguel wasn't talking to him.

* * *

"Before we close, I want to show you all something you might not have seen yet," Reverend Thompson said, holding up a newspaper. "It seems the younger members of our congregation have been at it again, and let me be the first to offer my sincerest congratulations and encouragement."

Jenna strained forward from her seat with the choir, but all she could see was the back side of the paper their pastor held up at the pulpit.

The reverend cleared his throat and proceeded to read. "This Halloween, when many will be thinking only of candy and parties, eight former classmates of deceased Clearwater Crossing High School student Kurt Englbehrt will be working to make a difference," he began, going on to read the entire article about Eight Prime.

"We could all learn a lesson from these young people," he said when he had finished. "Let me read now from the Book of James."

He looked down at his Bible and began reading again. " 'What good is it, my brothers, if a man claims to have faith but has no deeds? Can such faith save him? Suppose a brother or sister is without clothes and daily food.

" 'If one of you says to him, "Go, I wish you well; keep warm and well fed," but does nothing about his physical needs, what good is it? In the same way, faith by itself, if it is not accompanied by action, is dead.' "

Reverend Thompson looked up from the pulpit and smiled. "It would appear that faith is very much alive in the fine young people of our church. And I'd like to say how proud I am to know them."

After the service was over, Jenna rushed to put away her choir robe and find Peter. He was by their usual bench outside, along with Chris and Maura. The three of them were surrounded by a large group of parishioners.

"Anything you kids need, you just let me know," Mr. Riley was saying as Jenna wriggled through the crowd to Peter's side.

"Actually," said Peter, "we need chaperones for all three nights."

"Sign me up!" Mr. Riley commanded. "I'll be there."

"I can help you, Peter," another voice called out.

"Me too," said someone else. "I'd love to chaperone."

It was incredible. The smile on Jenna's face grew by degrees as the offers of support poured in from all sides. Peter scribbled names frantically on the back of a bulletin from that morning's service.

And then came the most amazing offer of all.

"You kids got a bus picked out yet?" Mr. Haig asked, removing a weather-beaten pipe from his lips.

Jenna and Peter exchanged startled glances. Mr. Haig was a middle-aged bachelor, a farmer who almost never spoke except to comment on the weather.

"No sir," Peter replied. "I'm afraid we need to save a lot more money before we can think about shopping."

Mr. Haig nodded thoughtfully. "I could check into that a bit, if you want. Could be I know a good used one coming up."

"That would be fantastic!" Jenna burst in. "Wouldn't it, Peter?"

Peter and Chris glanced briefly at each other, then turned to Mr. Haig.

"Absolutely," Peter said. "Neither Chris nor I really know all that much about buses. If you could point us at a good one, sir, that would be a major help."

Mr. Haig nodded, then put his hands in his pockets and wandered off.

"How exciting!" Jenna exclaimed. "I wonder what kind of bus it is."

"One that runs safely, I hope," said Chris. "Aside from that, I don't much care."

"Of course not," Jenna agreed, her spirits soaring as she considered the events of the last few minutes. "But don't you see? With the haunted house getting so much publicity, and now Mr. Haig checking out a bus for us . . . well, we could be a whole lot closer to reaching our goal than anybody realized!"

"What about a black cat?" Courtney mused. "Or a *tiger*. That would go better with my hair."

119

"Whatever," Nicole answered distractedly. She had enough costumes to worry about already without taking charge of Courtney's. She skimmed the list in her hand again, reading to herself as they wandered through the mall. *Plastic fangs, fake blood, black lipstick, black nail polish, bobby pins, red lipstick, press-on fingernails, a skeleton mask, hair spray—*

"Or maybe I should ditch the cat idea altogether," Courtney interrupted.

"Uh-huh. Whatever."

A ski mask, a hockey mask, a toy chain saw . . .

"Do they even make toy chain saws?" Nicole stopped reading long enough to ask. That item had been one of Ben's bright ideas.

Courtney looked astonished, which was always a bad sign. "What kind of psychos are you hanging out with?" she asked. "Toy chain saws? I'm sure!"

Nicole scratched out the chain saw. It was just as well, except now she'd have to think of something to replace it with.

"Let me see that list," Courtney demanded, snatching it and looking it over. "You can probably get most of this stuff at Walgreens," she said after she had read it. "The hockey mask I'd buy at a secondhand sports store. It'll be cheaper there than getting it new."

"And what about the skeleton mask?"

"That's costume store stuff," Courtney said disdainfully. "Or *maybe* the toy store. Really, Nicole, I thought you knew more about shopping."

Nicole took back her list and scanned it again. Courtney was right—she should have gone to the local drugstore and skipped the mall altogether. "Excuse me," she retorted, annoyed. "I have a few other things on my mind, is all."

"Yeah? How *is* Jesse, anyway?"

Nicole sighed, wondering when she'd learn to stop sparring with Courtney. She inevitably came out worse for the experience. "He's fine," she said shortly. The last thing she wanted was to discuss the way he'd told her to shut up the day before. Even if it *was* practically all she could think about.

"Uh-oh. Melanie back in the picture again?"

"No, not at all."

That, at least, was true. Nicole couldn't remember Melanie and Jesse talking together once the entire day before. Melanie had been so busy painting with Peter, in fact, that she'd barely had time for anyone else. *Which is perfect,* thought Nicole. *At least with Peter she can't do any harm.*

"I'd think you'd be a little more interested in helping me out, then," Courtney complained. "This is only the biggest party so far this year. I need a really cool costume."

"I *will* help you out. I'll drive us over to Walgreens."

Courtney rolled her eyes but followed along as Nicole changed directions in the mall and headed toward the exit. "I still can't believe you're going to miss Dennis's party for a stupid haunted house. I want you to go with me and Jeff."

"That party hadn't even been announced when I said I'd work at the haunted house," Nicole replied impatiently. "I don't know what you expect me to do about it now."

The party Courtney was so excited about was the biggest thing to hit the CCHS social scene so far that year. Dennis Peterson, one of the Wildcats, was putting it on. Everyone knew about it, everyone was invited, and so far it sounded as if everyone would be there, too. *Everyone but us*, Nicole grumbled to herself, imagining the members of Eight Prime slaving away in social obscurity. The situation was depressing enough without Courtney rubbing it in.

"Let your goody-goody friends take care of it without you," Courtney returned. "Ever since you joined the God Squad I hardly even see you anymore."

Lately when Courtney made cracks about the God Squad, Nicole wasn't sure if she was still referring to Jenna and Peter, or if she now meant all of Eight Prime. "Give me a break. The reason you don't see me is you're constantly with Jeff."

"All I'm saying is that ever since you started hanging out with those people, you're missing everything. I really want you to go to this party."

"And I want to go, all right? But there are things in life more important than parties."

The two friends stared at each other.

Did that just come out of my mouth? Nicole wondered, shocked.

And then she remembered how she had prayed for the ability to remember that life was bigger than parties, and dates, and diets, and the other superficial things that tended to obsess her.

She smiled wonderingly to herself. Maybe someone had been listening.

Nine

"Hi, Leah!" some guy Leah didn't know called out.

"Hey, Leah. How's it going?" another strange voice asked her as she made her way down the hall Monday morning.

"Um, fine." She smiled uncomfortably in the direction the greetings had come from, not even sure who had spoken.

"Hi, Leah." A couple of girls she'd met the week before waved, then gave her a serious once-over, as if memorizing her outfit.

She nodded in their direction, still weaving through hallway traffic.

I hate this, she thought. Wherever she went these days, strange guys flirted and girls stared openly. *I used to walk around school practically unnoticed. Now people are judging my clothes, my hair, my makeup. I'm sick of being a U.S. Girl!*

But if she dropped out now, she could kiss her chance at the scholarship good-bye. *The worst dam-*

age is probably already done anyway, she mused. *Everyone already knows I won. Besides, Nicole and Miguel would have a fit if I quit.*

Leah reached her locker, spun out the combination, and began selecting books. She understood why Nicole was so wrapped up in the whole U.S. Girls thing, but Miguel? What was the deal with that? All Leah knew for sure was that every time she even mentioned quitting he squawked as loudly as Nicole.

Maybe he gets some kind of secret ego boost out of dating a model, she thought disgustedly, slamming her locker door. The sound rang out and was absorbed into the cacophony of other noises around her. *On the other hand, if that were true, it seems like he'd want somebody to know about it.*

She sighed as she headed off to class. After Eight Prime had interrupted her and Miguel's argument on Saturday, the subject of them getting together on Sunday hadn't come up again. She hadn't seen him, hadn't met his mother, hadn't told anyone they were a couple . . . He hadn't even called her. Of course, he never did. Mr. Talkative hated the telephone.

Well, at least we're going to the homecoming dance together, she thought.

Then a second thought made her smile. *There's no way Miguel's renting a tuxedo and getting dressed in that* little house without his mother finding out. *If she knows he's going to a formal, she's bound to want pictures of him and his date.*

Her smile grew even larger. *Miguel del Rios, you may have just cooked your own goose.*

The first thing Leah planned to do when she saw her secret boyfriend was make good and sure that their homecoming date was still on.

"Peter! Jenna!" Nicole called, running to catch them on the front lawn after school on Monday. "Wait for me!"

They stopped, and Nicole hurriedly closed the distance between them.

"So, are we meeting at your house tomorrow or at the warehouse?" she asked Peter. "I totally forgot."

"The warehouse. Otherwise everyone would just have to drive two places, right?"

"Oh. Right. And what time is it again?"

"Six o'clock." Peter was beginning to look at her strangely.

"I know, I know. I spaced," Nicole admitted. "There's just so much going on . . . all those costumes . . ."

"How's that going?" Jenna asked.

"Don't ask!" Nicole exclaimed, happy that someone had. "I spent all day yesterday running to different stores trying to get things we needed. Then I had to work on the overall plan of who'd dress how and where they'd hide and what they'd do. This whole plan thing you guys wanted . . . I really don't know what I'm doing. I mean, this isn't a play, right? So why are we assigning roles? Why can't everyone just pick a hiding place and jump out screaming now and then?"

"That sounds like a plan to me," Peter teased. "Maybe you're better at this than you think."

"Yeah, right." Nicole wanted to discuss it further, but Jenna interrupted.

"Hey, there's Courtney," said Jenna, waving.

Nicole looked over to see Courtney and Jeff crossing the lawn in their direction. Nicole waved too, fully expecting Courtney to alter her course when she realized she was headed straight for the God Squad. To Nicole's surprise, however, Jeff waved back, and the couple hurried forward to join them.

"Hi, Peter! Hi, Jenna!" Jeff greeted them enthusiastically. "Hey, Nicole. How's it going?"

Nicole felt her eyebrows shoot up. This was unexpected. *Could it be?*

"It's going good, Jeff," said Peter. "How are things with you?"

Nicole almost laughed out loud. *It is! Courtney's too-cool boyfriend knows the dreaded Peter and Jenna.*

"Hey, I saw that article about your haunted house in the paper," Jeff said. "I was wondering . . . I mean, if it's not too late . . . well, maybe Courtney and I can help somehow."

"That would be great!" Peter told him. "We'd love to have your help."

Nicole was trying hard to make eye contact with Courtney, but her best friend wouldn't look at her. Instead her eyes were fixed stubbornly on an imaginary spot in the distance.

"So, what can we do?" Jeff asked. "It would be fun if we could work inside, scaring people."

"You can do that if you want to," Peter said. "You just need to get with Nicole here. She's in charge of all the costumes."

"And what about until then? Do you have anything left to do before you open up on Thursday?"

Jenna laughed. "Tons of stuff!"

"As a matter of fact," said Peter, "we'll be working on our sets tomorrow night at the warehouse. It's kind of an Eight Prime meeting, too, but we're mostly going to work. You'd both be welcome to come."

"Great!" said Jeff. "What time should we be there?"

"Six o'clock, or whenever you can." Peter smiled. "It'll be great to have a chance to find out what you've been up to lately, Jeff."

Jeff nodded and his straight black hair brushed across his forehead. "I'm looking forward to catching up too. I'm really glad I saw that article."

Jeff turned to Courtney, who had yet to say a

thing. "Isn't this going to be more fun than that stupid party?" he demanded.

"You're not missing the party!" Nicole blurted out before Courtney could reply. "No! I don't believe it!"

"You don't have to help on Halloween night if you want to go to Dennis's party, Jeff," said Peter. "We've got plenty of other people. You could just work on Thursday and Friday."

For the first time, Courtney looked at them, her green eyes full of hope, but Jeff shook his head decisively.

"No way! We'd much rather hang out with you guys and help those little kids. Isn't that right, Courtney?"

"Um, sure," Courtney said, her voice half strangled by lack of conviction.

Nicole could barely keep from laughing. Under other circumstances, she might have felt some sympathy for her friend, but this was such sweet justice that she could hardly keep still. Not only was Courtney missing her big Halloween party, her hot new flame was obviously old buds with the God Squad. It was too good to let pass, and in the end Nicole couldn't resist.

"But I thought you really wanted to go to that party, Courtney," she said innocently. "It seems a shame to miss it after all the planning you did for your saloon-girl costume. . . ."

Jeff immediately turned to his girlfriend. "Is that true?" he asked, his expression confused. "I thought you said working at the haunted house was fine with—"

"It is," Courtney assured him hurriedly. She turned to face Nicole, a warning glint in her eyes.

"After all, Nicole," she said haughtily, "there's more to life than parties."

Melanie heard a gentle cough behind her as she rummaged through her locker, and her heart sank like a brick. Even before she turned around, she knew what she would find.

"Uh, hi, Melanie," Sammy Watts mumbled shyly, his cheeks already flushed pink with embarrassment. Behind him the after-school rush had nearly cleared out of the hallway, leaving them alone.

"Hi, Sammy." She knew him vaguely from second-period English, where he sat in the seat behind hers. He'd always seemed like a nice kid—*kid* being the key word. He was a sophomore, but, with his unruly brown curls and hairless pink cheeks, he could have easily passed for a junior-high student.

Don't ask me, she thought, putting all her mental energy into somehow changing his mind. *Do not ask me*. She didn't want to hurt his feelings, but experience told her what was coming next.

"I was, uh, wondering, Melanie," he said awkwardly. "I mean, a girl like you probably gets asked by everyone . . . But then I thought, 'Hey, *maybe*. You never know.' I mean, if everyone thought that way . . ."

He's going to do it. He's going to ask me. Melanie sighed and readied her excuse while Sammy fumbled to the point.

"The thing is, the homecoming dance is coming up, and I was wondering . . . I mean, if you would . . ."

"I'm sorry, Sammy," she broke in, anxious to end his suffering. "It's nice of you to think of me, but I'm going with someone else."

Sammy nodded. "Of course you are. What was I thinking?"

Melanie smiled and shouldered her backpack. "I'm not *that* in demand. Hey, maybe I'll see you there, though. We can catch a dance together."

"Really?" His face lit up all over. "Okay. Cool."

Melanie hurried away through the hall, wishing homecoming were already over. At least Sammy had seemed satisfied with the promise of a dance. Not everyone took rejection so well.

Maybe I should have said yes, she thought as she ran down the outdoor steps. *I suppose I could do worse. Sammy probably wouldn't get drunk or try to grope me on the dance floor.*

For a moment she almost reconsidered. The problem was that she didn't *know* Sammy. Not really. It was kind of surprising that he'd even asked

131

her. She was positive why he had though. It was the same inane reason they all asked her out: because she was Melanie Andrews.

Whoever that is. She reached the bus stop and sat on a bench.

On the other hand, she was going to have to go to the dance with someone. It would be a relief to settle on a date so she didn't have to keep making excuses.

But who? She couldn't think of anyone.

I suppose Jesse would take me if I asked him. That would mean making up with him, though. And, if he ran true to form, they'd be fighting again by the end of the night. *I wish I knew a guy I could ask just to go as my friend. It would be so nice to have a friend like that. The same way Jenna has Peter.*

Melanie wondered if those two would go together. *They do everything else as a team*, she thought. On the other hand, this was a major formal. It was possible they'd take dates. But, hard as she tried, she couldn't imagine who they'd go with. She never saw either of them with anyone else. If Peter didn't take Jenna, Melanie had no idea who he'd ask. He could take anyone. He could take her.

She cocked a speculative brow. *Come to think of it, Peter would be the perfect date.*

Ten

"Can't you hurry, Caitlin?" Jenna asked impatiently, sticking her head through the doorway of Caitlin and Sarah's room Tuesday night. "We're already late."

"Sorry." Caitlin was on her hands and knees, rooting around beneath her bed. "I know my down jacket's under here somewhere."

"We're going to be inside!"

Caitlin looked up. "I'm pretty sure that warehouse isn't heated."

She may have a point, Jenna admitted. While Caitlin resumed her search, Jenna ran back upstairs for a coat of her own.

I wonder if Peter is already there, she thought as she thundered up the two flights of stairs. He had offered to drive her, but she had wanted to bring Caitlin again, and Caitlin had been far from ready when he'd called. The girls had decided to drive themselves. *Tonight I'm definitely going to work with Peter*, Jenna promised herself, looking forward to

133

spending some time with him. *Someone else can carry Melanie's stupid ladder!*

At last Caitlin was ready. Jenna drove them through the dark streets in a hurry, her mind full of Peter and the haunted house, but Caitlin didn't seem to mind the lack of conversation. Before long they pulled up at the ComAm warehouse.

In the dark the place actually looked a little spooky. The low, windowless building hugged the dark ground, only a pale, uncertain light filtering through the partially open front door. Behind the building and overhead, ancient oak trees spread their gnarled branches in eerie silhouette against the rising moon. And all around them the dry rustle of October leaves filled the chill night breeze. Jenna shivered under her coat as she and Caitlin hurried across the black pavement.

Inside the storehouse, though, the scariest thing was how much work remained to be done before they could open Thursday night. Everyone was running from task to task, trying to do five things at once and not actually finishing anything. Partition walls in various states of completion had been erected everywhere—some slathered with a single drippy coat of black paint and some still bare wood. Jenna and Caitlin wandered toward the back, assessing the situation.

Jesse, Miguel, and Jeff were hammering away at a few last partitions, while Courtney and Nicole hung yards and yards of cheap black gauze in the gaps between them, forming a maze of small rooms and connecting halls. Leah was creating tombstones and the false front of a crypt from painted blocks of Styrofoam. Ben wandered by them, struggling to figure out the cotton spiderwebs. And, at the very end of the building, Jenna could see Peter's blond head bobbing up over the partitions as he stood painting on the ladder. She hurried forward until, through a gap in the makeshift walls, she glimpsed Melanie painting at his side. Jenna froze where she stood. She was too late. Melanie and Peter were already working together again.

"So, what do you want to do?" she asked her sister. It was hard to keep the disappointment out of her voice, but Jenna was determined not to blame Caitlin for Peter's choice of partner. *On the other hand, if Caitlin had simply been ready on time . . .*

"We could paint," Caitlin suggested. "There are still a lot of bare walls."

Jenna thought only a second. "Good idea," she agreed. "Let's paint." There was no reason they couldn't all work together.

She and Caitlin walked to the end of the warehouse. "Need any help?" Jenna called up to Peter. "You've got two volunteers here."

"Oh, good!" Melanie answered for him. "There are some partitions way over in the corner that don't have any paint at all on them yet." With the

135

paintbrush in her hand, Melanie pointed to the opposite side of the warehouse. "They all need to be painted black. You can take one of those buckets of paint and grab some rollers and drop cloths and whatever else you need."

Caitlin began picking up supplies, but Jenna didn't budge. "I thought we could work together," she said, in a reasonably calm tone of voice. "Wouldn't that be more fun?"

"Sure," Peter said, finally glancing down from his ladder. "But we'll finish faster if we split up. We don't have a lot of time left, you know."

"We can't all four paint one wall, anyway," Melanie added apologetically. "We'd just be in each other's way."

"Fine," Jenna said abruptly, grabbing a roller and drop cloth. "Come on, Caitlin." They trudged across the building to the walls Melanie had assigned them and began painting in total silence.

Melanie's right; we can't all paint one wall, Jenna told herself over and over as her roller splashed paint in every direction. But it didn't do any good. She was still furious. If they couldn't all paint together, how come *Melanie* got to paint with Peter? *Because you were late and they'd already started*. Her head knew it was true, but her heart refused to believe it.

Peter would rather paint with Melanie than you, a nagging little voice insisted. And no matter how hard Jenna tried to ignore it, it wouldn't take a break.

"I'm going to go get another paintbrush," she announced suddenly, dropping her roller into its sloppy black pan.

Caitlin nodded, not bothering to point out that they weren't using the two brushes they already had. Jenna hurried back to Peter's corner of the storehouse.

"Hi! It's me again!" she announced brightly at the base of his ladder.

"What's up?" he asked. "Forget something?"

"Actually, yes. We need another paintbrush." She picked one up.

"That's weird," Melanie commented, turning away from the dead vines she was painting to check her pile of painting equipment. "If you guys don't already have two, then one's gone missing. I must have left it around here somewhere."

"Hmm," Jenna said.

"I'd better go find it before it dries out." Melanie set her wet brush on the lid of her brown paint can and wandered off, her eyes scanning the floor.

Jenna knew she only had a few minutes. "Hey, Peter, can you come down here, please?" she asked.

Peter looked down from the ladder. "What for?"

She could tell he didn't want to. "Just come on down, okay?"

He stepped down reluctantly. "What's the matter, Jenna? I'm kind of busy here."

"Yeah. That's the problem," Jenna said, careful

to keep her voice low. "You're always kind of busy—just not with me."

"What's that supposed to mean?"

"Saturday you worked with Melanie all day. And now you're doing it again. What about me?"

"What about you? You're working with Caitlin, aren't you?"

Don't be so dense! Jenna wanted to shout. Melanie would be back any second.

"I wanted to work with you," she told him. "We never do anything together anymore."

"That's not true." Peter's tone signaled his growing irritation. "We've had lunch together both days this week."

"Yeah, with Ben. That doesn't count."

Peter shook his head. "I honestly don't even know what you want. Do you want me to ask Melanie to go work with Caitlin, so I can paint with you instead?"

"No," Jenna said sullenly. That was exactly what she wanted.

"Then what's the problem?"

"I just think . . . well . . . I feel like you'd rather be with Melanie than me." She held her breath, waiting for the explosion, the heated denials.

But Peter only rolled his eyes. "That's so ridiculous, I don't even know what to say."

"Try saying it isn't true!"

"Of course it isn't. You *know* it isn't. I don't know how you could think that."

Jenna was about to tell him exactly how when Melanie reappeared.

"Well, I can't find the other paintbrush," she said. "It'll probably show up eventually, with the paint dried as hard as cement."

She shrugged, but Jenna could tell it was really bothering her. "I'll, uh, go double-check our stuff to make sure we don't have it after all," she said guiltily.

"Do you want me to come with you?" Melanie offered.

"No. No, that's okay." Jenna turned around and hurried back toward Caitlin, her mind filled with confusion.

So Peter's painting with Melanie, she told herself, blinking to keep back tears. *That doesn't mean he likes her better—that's just how things worked out.*

He'd *said* he didn't like her better anyway. But his voice hadn't exactly rung with conviction.

Jenna passed Leah and Miguel, who were working together now, but she was much too preoccupied by the situation with Peter to pay them any attention. She reached her station, picked up her roller, and started splattering paint around again, grinding her teeth as Melanie's laughter echoed through the warehouse.

139

Half of her wanted to march back over there and confront Peter, but the other half was afraid of looking like more of a fool than she already did. The next peal of giggles decided her, though. Jenna couldn't take any more.

"I've got to give this paintbrush back to Melanie," she told Caitlin, grabbing the unused brush she'd so recently borrowed. Without waiting for an answer, she started back toward Peter.

This is so stupid, she argued with herself as she wove through the sets. *I don't even know why I'm doing this.* She didn't know why her pulse was racing, or her stomach felt empty, or her eyes kept filling with water, either. She only knew that she didn't like what was happening. More precisely, she was starting to actively *dislike* the sight of Melanie and Peter together.

If the mere idea hadn't been so ridiculous, she'd have almost believed she was jealous.

"I guess that's all we can do tonight." Miguel set his hammer on the floor and stood up, stretching his tired back. It was late, and he and Peter were the last two people working at the haunted house. "At least all the walls are up and braced now."

"We're almost done with everything." Peter looked around with an appraising eye. "All the construction is done, and all the black background painting. It's really just details now. A little more decorating, some scenery painting . . ."

"Don't forget about the sound and lighting," said Miguel.

"Oh yeah. Do you want to meet me here after school tomorrow so that we can take care of that? Ben gave me the key."

Miguel smiled. "Did he give you that groovy key ring, too?"

"No. I managed to convince him I didn't need that," Peter said with a chuckle.

"Sometimes I wonder about that guy."

Peter locked the front door, and the two of them walked down to the street and their separate cars. With a short, friendly beep of his horn, Peter drove off, but Miguel idled at the curb, waiting for his defroster to work.

Eight Prime was pretty fun tonight, he thought as his pitted windshield cleared. *And I'm sure glad Leah's in a better mood.* She had seemed like her old self again, in fact: happy and talkative and full of whispered plans for the homecoming dance when she thought no one was looking.

"I'm going to be wearing a strapless dress," she'd told him, letting her lips just brush his ear. "So you'd better get me a wrist corsage."

"Huh?" he'd teased in reply. "You lost me back at 'strapless.' "

Miguel smiled now as he pulled his car out into the street. He was starting to look forward to this homecoming formal more than he'd expected.

There were no lights on inside the del Rios house when Miguel parked out in front. As late as it was, he'd expected that. His mom and Rosa would have gone to sleep long before in the small bedroom they shared. Miguel hated that his mother didn't have her own room, but there were only two and he and Rosa couldn't exactly share. He crept quietly up the front walkway, then eased the front door open and slipped silently into the dark living room.

"Oh!" His mother jumped to her feet, popping up only a few feet away. "Miguel, you scared me!" she whispered reproachfully. "I didn't hear you walk up."

She had been kneeling near the end of the sofa. In the dim glow of the streetlight filtering in through the window, Miguel saw the rosary dangling from her fingers.

"Oh, and you didn't scare me a bit," he whispered back sarcastically, his heart pounding up near his throat.

"Sorry. I couldn't sleep, and I didn't want to wake Rosa."

The rosary suddenly took on new significance. "Is everything all right?" he asked nervously.

"Yes, fine. I'm fine, don't worry."

"Then why are you out here praying rosaries at this hour?" His fear had receded quickly, leaving anger in its place. "In fact, why pray them at all? It's a total waste of time."

"I'll thank you to watch your mouth." His mother's voice held a hint of steel. He had made her angry too. "God hears you, Miguel."

Miguel could think of five different comebacks, each more sacrilegious than the last, but he couldn't bring himself to say any of those things to his mother. In the end he settled for leaving the room.

"He *might* hear me—if he ever bothered to listen," he muttered as he shut his bedroom door. "She ought to know by now that he doesn't."

Eleven

" 'There's a time for us . . .' " Jenna's voice lifted out over the music as the CCHS choir practiced for its Thanksgiving recital. "Someday" from *West Side Story* was Jenna's duet with Ron Holder. She usually loved to sing it, but that Wednesday she mouthed through the lyrics on autopilot, barely hearing herself and not listening to Ron at all.

If Peter and I are going to the homecoming dance, I need to buy a dress, she thought as she held a high note. *I wish he'd hurry up and ask me.*

It was very strange that he'd let things go so long without saying anything. Usually he asked her to go with him as soon as a dance was announced—as friends, of course. But he still hadn't said a word, and Jenna was getting worried.

I should just ask him, she thought, swinging into her second verse. *But he always asks me. Still . . . I guess there isn't any reason I can't ask him. He's probably just assuming we'll go together. That's it, I'll bet . . . Unless he's thinking of asking someone else!*

144

Jenna's heart lurched at the possibility. *Would he? And if so, who? Melanie?*

No, that's silly, she reassured herself hurriedly. *But maybe someone in one of his classes—*

"Cut! Stop! *Please* stop," her choir teacher, Mr. Evans, yelled suddenly, right in the middle of the finale. "Jenna, do you feel all right today?"

"Huh? Uh, sure."

"You're certain you don't have a cold? Your ears aren't blocked or anything?"

She could feel her cheeks heating up. This line of questioning couldn't go anywhere good.

"No." Her voice was barely a whisper.

"Then why can't you hear how flat you are? You're so far off, it's making my molars ache."

"I—I'm sorry, Mr. Evans," Jenna stammered, mortified. She was used to being praised for her singing. To be told she was singing terribly was a totally new experience for her—one she could have done without. "I guess I wasn't concentrating."

"Well, *start* concentrating. *Please.* Let me hear only the first phrase." He banged out on the piano the notes he wanted her to sing. "Go."

Jenna sang it a cappella, taking special care over every note.

Mr. Evans grunted. "Again."

She sang, praying the rest of the choir couldn't hear the growing desperation in her voice.

"That's more like it!" Mr. Evans exclaimed. "That's the Jenna Conrad I know. Tell whoever that other impostor was not to come back to my class."

The rest of the choir tittered with amusement as their teacher turned back to Ron. "From the top!"

Ron started the song from the beginning while Jenna waited tensely to come in on the second verse. Her hands shook from Mr. Evans's casual cruelty, and her nervousness increased note by note.

Don't think about Peter. Don't think about the homecoming dance, she told herself hurriedly as the teacher cued her in. *Just concentrate on singing!"*

"You've got to be kidding," Melanie protested, handing a wrinkled sheet of notes back to Angela Maldonado. "This is what we're doing now?"

She had been back at school exactly two weeks that Wednesday, but this was the first cheerleading practice her doctor had cleared her to attend since her head injury. And had things ever changed for the worse!

Ms. Carson had been relieved of duty as the squad's advisor, and the school still hadn't assigned another one. In the meantime, the cheerleaders had to practice at the edge of the field while the Wildcats worked out so Coach Davis could keep an eye on them. All this Melanie had known. What she hadn't known was exactly what the coach had them doing.

The paper she'd just handed back to Angela contained a list of calisthenics to be completed at every practice—before they did anything else! Melanie remembered hearing some griping about the new exercises the coach had added to their workout, but she obviously hadn't paid enough attention.

I should have made more of an effort to hang out with the girls at lunchtime and get caught up on the gossip, she thought. But eating with Vanessa had never been her favorite thing, and lately she'd been busy with Eight Prime.

"How are we supposed to do all that and practice cheering, too?" Melanie asked Angela. "If I finish that list, I'll be too tired to move."

Angela glanced nervously toward Vanessa, as if afraid to say anything. The cheerleading captain was sitting with a few other girls on the sideline bench, safely out of earshot.

"I think that's the idea," Angela admitted. "By the time we get through all that, there's usually only time for a couple of cheers and maybe one dance. No flips allowed, no handsprings . . . no cartwheels, even."

Melanie shook her head, amazed.

"But it won't be very much longer," Angela added hopefully, with another nervous glance at Vanessa. "We're supposed to get our new coach any day."

Tiffany Barrett came into view then, sauntering across the grass to join them. "Ah, well, here's another fun afternoon!" she called in a sarcastic voice. "Can we do extra jumping jacks today, Vanessa? Can we, huh?" She tossed her gym bag onto the grass at their squad leader's feet.

"Shut up, Tiffany," Vanessa snarled. She rose from the bench and clapped her hands for everyone to form up. The squad took positions as if going to cheer, then Vanessa made the call. "Fifty toe touches. Go! One, two, three . . ."

Melanie stood and watched in astonishment as the other girls counted off reps.

Vanessa suddenly noticed Melanie wasn't moving. "Stop!" she shouted. Everyone froze halfway to their toes, then straightened up to watch.

"Listen, Melanie," Vanessa said sharply. "If you're not well enough to be at practice yet, then by all means go home. But don't just stand there like a zombie, messing everyone up."

"Like you could mess *this* up," Melanie heard Sue Tilford whisper.

"Oh, sure. How come *we* all have to do this crap and Melanie gets to go home?" Tiffany demanded. "It's her fault we're doing it at all!"

"Shut up, Tiffany," Tanya Jeffries growled. "When you get knocked unconscious, you can cut practice too."

I'd like to knock her unconscious, Melanie thought, temporarily distracted.

"We haven't practiced the spirit pyramid once

since Melanie fell," Tiffany complained, unabashed. "And now that we're assigned to Coach Davis, we can't practice anything else, either."

"I told you it's only temporary," Vanessa said impatiently. "You're such a bunch of whiners!"

But Melanie wasn't listening anymore. Tiffany's comment about the spirit pyramid had reminded her of something.

"You know, Vanessa," she broke in. "I met a girl from Red River on Friday, and she said their squad has never done a flip onto the spirit pyramid. She said the whole idea was crazy, in fact . . . that their coach would never let them do something so dangerous."

All eyes turned toward Vanessa, who did her best to pretend not to notice. "I heard something else," she said haughtily.

"Yeah? Well, what exactly did you hear? And who did you hear it from?"

"I . . . I don't remember. Exactly. It was just something . . . that they were doing it. That's what I heard." Vanessa's close-set eyes met Melanie's only a moment before they glanced away, toward the Wildcats at the end of the field.

"But who told you that?" Melanie persisted.

"Some girl. It was . . . a girl," Vanessa said evasively. "I don't remember her name."

"You mean you don't want to tell it to me," Melanie said suspiciously.

"No. I just . . . can we drop it? So I'm not perfect—what do you want from me? Blood?"

Melanie blinked at the unexpected admission. "Sure, Vanessa. We can drop it," she said slowly.

But for the first time since her head hit the pavement, Melanie found herself wondering if her injury was more than an accident.

"This is working pretty well," Miguel said, flipping down the flap of black fabric that concealed Leah's boom box. Between everyone in Eight Prime, they had collected six of the powerful tape players, and Peter had rounded up a cassette tape of spooky sounds for each one. Creaks, groans, screams, and wails filled the storehouse from six invisible sources. In combination with the eerie, minimal lighting he and Peter had rigged, the effect was surprisingly scary. "This place is actually starting to creep me out."

Peter nodded. "When all of us get in here in costume and start jumping out everywhere, it ought to be even scarier."

"It'll scare the little kids, all right. I'm not so sure about the big ones."

"Wait and see," Peter said confidently. "Being afraid is only ten percent related to what's actually happening—the other ninety percent all happens in your head." He smiled as he looked around the haunted warehouse. "A person with imagination could terrify himself in here."

Maybe he's right, Miguel thought. *In any event, it ought to be worth five bucks.* "I hope we get a lot of people."

"I think we'll get a ton of people. Everyone at school has been asking me about it ever since that article in Sunday's paper. I have a feeling we'll be busy." Peter lifted the curtain and made an adjustment to the sound on Leah's boom box. "Which reminds me, are your parents chaperoning on any of the nights?"

"My mom can't."

"Well, what about your dad?"

Miguel hesitated. "My, uh . . . my father's dead." He stumbled over the words, but in a way saying them was a relief. He wanted Eight Prime to know.

"I'm sorry." Peter seemed genuinely upset. "Why didn't you say something before?"

Miguel tried to smile, but his face felt numb. At least he wasn't crying. "I don't much like to talk about it."

"Sure. I understand."

Do you? thought Miguel. He doubted it.

"So, I guess your mom has to stay home and watch the house, right?"

"Sort of."

Peter looked at him expectantly.

"She's sort of sick," Miguel added reluctantly.

"I'm sorry," Peter said again. "I hope it's nothing serious."

Miguel shrugged.

"What's the matter with her?"

"It's . . . nothing. She'll be fine." He said what he wanted to believe.

"But if she can't leave the house—"

"She can leave the house, Peter. She just gets tired easily. She can't stand around a lot."

"Is there anything I can do? Or my mom? Some of the ladies at church have a group that cooks for the sick—"

"We don't need any more charity!" Miguel could feel his temper slipping, and he worked to rein it back in. "She's just . . . she needs a kidney transplant, all right? I haven't told anyone, because I don't want the whole world to know, but that's the way it is. She won't get any better until she gets a kidney."

"But our church—"

"Unless your church is passing out body parts, they can't do a thing, okay?"

"We can pray. I'm going to pray for her every night, Miguel, and ask God to make her well."

It was too much. Miguel tried to keep his mouth shut, his teeth clenched tightly together, but he'd been holding back too long. The force of his unspoken feelings broke down every barrier.

"Yeah, that's perfect," he said sarcastically. "Pray for my mother. Pray for her the way you prayed for Kurt, and I'll hope things go better this time."

"Miguel, I—"

"Don't you know that he can't hear you? He either can't hear, or he doesn't listen—the end result's the same."

"You're wrong," Peter said with conviction.

"Oh, I used to be like you," Miguel sneered. "I used to believe in a god who answered prayers. But then my father got cancer and died. There's no way I'll believe in God now. A god who won't take care of innocent people doesn't *deserve* my belief!"

Peter didn't reply. His eyes had dropped halfway closed against the assault. In a rush, Miguel realized that he'd probably permanently offended him. Almost as suddenly, he knew that he didn't want to lose Peter's friendship.

"I . . . look, whatever, Peter. I know you believe in God, and I know you just wanted to help me. I wasn't trying . . . I didn't mean . . ."

Peter waved off his apology. "No problem. I get the feeling that's been building a long time."

Miguel shrugged and began picking up tools, eager to call it a night.

But Peter didn't move.

"You know, Miguel," he said slowly, "I guess I don't blame you for how you feel, not after what you've been through. But . . . well, you must see the contradiction in what you're saying."

Miguel stopped working. "What do you mean?"

"I mean, you can't not believe in God and be mad at him too. And you're obviously pretty mad at him. So . . ."

Peter was right. The realization burst over Miguel with the intensity of something he should have seen long ago. He *was* mad at God. No, he was *furious*. Every time he thought about him, he wanted to break something, to tear something down, to scream, to kick, to demand some justice.

Could he be this outraged if in his heart he didn't still believe?

Twelve

Jenna and Peter pulled up in front of the haunted house at the same time as Leah and Miguel, and Jesse with the rest of Eight Prime. The moment school had let out that Thursday, they'd all run to the student parking lot and driven to the warehouse.

"I can't believe we're opening tonight!" Jenna exclaimed as she got out of the car. "I hope we're ready."

"I think we are," Peter said. "But it's always good to double-check."

Jenna stuck close to her friend as they walked to the front door. She had finally managed to ride with Peter, and she intended to work with him, too.

Ben had just unlocked the door when another car rolled up. It was Caitlin, who'd come to help them. Everyone else went in to do their last-minute tasks, but Jenna and Peter waited outside.

"Hey, Cat," Jenna greeted her sister, "I didn't know you were coming tonight."

"Not *tonight*," Caitlin corrected nervously. "Not

when you open for all those people. Just this afternoon."

"Well, come on in," Peter said. "We were just about to take the tour and see if anything needs to be fixed."

Inside, someone had switched on the special lights and sounds. Wails and clanking chains filled the entry area and a dull, diffused light sifted through motes of dust and heavy cobwebs. Yards of black gauze, the black ticket-taking furniture, and the tattered guide ropes gave the entry the look of an ancient theater lobby in the last stages of disrepair. Leaving the front door open, the three of them continued on their way.

Leah and Miguel were working on the crypt, making sure that the fake stone blocks that surrounded its entrance were well secured to the wall the entry opening had been cut in. Jenna walked by them into the cobweb-strewn interior, where an open coffin made of rough boards the guys had knocked together held the center stage. Miguel's job was to climb inside and lie very still; then, when people stopped to look at him, he was supposed to snap into a sitting position and yell. Jenna shivered to imagine how scary that would be. Especially at night, when it was even darker inside.

They moved on through the next few rooms until they got to the one with the strobe light. Melanie was at work in there, touching up the white-and-black checkerboards painted on the walls. When the strobe light was on, a person walking through the room seemed to be moving in jerky slow motion. It wasn't that scary in itself, but it got scarier when people were in a hurry.

In the next room, Ben and Nicole were stuffing some old clothes with crumpled-up newspapers.

"What are you doing?" Jenna asked curiously.

"Last-minute inspiration," Nicole explained. "I thought we could put these dummies in the rooms that aren't as scary. In the dark, people will be freaking out trying to decide if they're real or not. They won't want to get too close, either, just in case they are."

"Good idea!" Peter said approvingly. "And you're right—after they get jumped at a couple of times, they won't be taking any chances."

The trio walked through a couple more rooms to the exit at the other end, then wound back through to the front. "Everything looks great!" Jenna said. "I don't even know what to work on."

"We could go help Ben and Nicole with those dummies," Peter suggested. "Or find out what Jesse's doing."

"I'm already done," Jesse announced, walking out from behind one of the makeshift walls with a hammer in his hand. "I was just double-checking to make sure there weren't any nails sticking out anywhere."

"Good idea," Jenna said with a shudder. "It would be awful if any of the blood in here wasn't fake."

Nicole joined them an instant later. "Are all of your costumes ready?" she asked anxiously. "You all have everything you need?"

"Yes, for the millionth time." Jesse rolled his eyes. "I think we can dress ourselves, Nicole."

Nicole bristled and was about to reply when a whimpering at the front door caught the group's attention. A stray dog had come to the open doorway. Its dirty, matted hair clung dully to skeletal ribs, and it had the beaten, cringing look of an animal that had been abused and abandoned. As Jenna watched, it tucked its sore-covered tail between its trembling hind legs and skittered inside, sniffing the floor for scraps.

"Oh, gross!" Nicole cried. "It probably has rabies."

"Someone get it out of here," Melanie echoed, walking up behind them.

Jesse looked around, then grabbed a crumpled old lunch bag from a corner. He fired it at the intruder, striking it in the flank. "Go on!" he shouted. "Get!"

Jenna expected the dog to flee in terror. Instead it cringed low to the concrete floor, whining and sniffing longingly at the brown paper bag that had once held food.

Jesse took the animal's unforeseen persistence as a challenge. "Go on!" he yelled again, advancing on the dog with heavy, stomping steps. "Shoo! Get out of here!"

"Stop it, Jesse!" a strong voice rang out. "Can't you see the poor thing is just hungry and lonely? Leave it alone right now."

Jesse stopped in his tracks, and Jenna's jaw dropped open. The speaker was Caitlin! The rest of the group watched in astonishment as she moved slowly but confidently toward the abandoned animal, her hand outstretched, her tone soft and soothing. "Here, dog. Come here, sweetie."

The dog came willingly, wriggling all over with joy. "That's a good girl," Caitlin purred, squatting down beside it and petting its filthy head. She removed a wadded Kleenex from her pocket and wiped tenderly at the congealed trails of mucus that ran from its eyes. "Good girl!" The dog whimpered a little, then tried to bury its face into Caitlin's bent knees, as if to hide in their shelter. Caitlin petted and whispered to it, then suddenly stood up.

"I'm taking it home," she announced, turning to Jenna. "You don't really need me here, and the poor thing's starving. I'm taking it home and giving it something to eat."

"In Mom's car?" Jenna blurted out, astonished. "Are you sure?"

"Of course I'm sure." The bold way Caitlin was acting made her seem like a total stranger. "You're still coming home for dinner before you open up tonight, right?"

Jenna nodded mutely.

"Fine. I'll see you then." Caitlin turned and strode from the warehouse, the filthy mutt trotting at her heels.

"Wow," Peter muttered under his breath. "I never knew Caitlin had that kind of backbone."

She doesn't, Jenna thought, still in a state of amazement. Her sister's behavior couldn't have been more unexpected. She watched as if paralyzed while Caitlin lifted the dog into the back of Mrs. Conrad's station wagon.

I hope Mom doesn't freak out when she sees that animal in her car, Jenna thought worriedly, wanting things to go well for Caitlin's sake. Her mom wasn't exactly a dog lover to begin with—the Conrads had never owned one—and that particular canine looked as if it might be carrying the plague. Jenna could only imagine her mom's reaction when Caitlin marched into the kitchen with her scraggly new pal and announced she was going to feed it.

"Maybe I ought to go with her," she said.

Peter smiled broadly, well aware of her mother's dislike of dogs. "Why? Do you feel lucky?"

"You're right," Jenna murmured, hurriedly abandoning the idea. "Caitlin's on her own."

"This is so cool!" Leah said excitedly as the Rosenthals drove slowly past the haunted house. "I'm glad you decided to come for the opening."

Mr. Rosenthal parked at the curb about a block away from the warehouse to leave room for other cars. "I wish we could have helped on the other nights, too," he said, "but between work and trick-or-treaters . . ."

"I *might* be able to get someone to take my seminar tomorrow night," Leah's mother offered. "Half my students will cut class anyway with all the parties going on."

"No. One night's enough," Leah assured them. "We have plenty of chaperones. I mostly just wanted you both to see it."

And to finally meet Miguel, she added to herself as the three of them walked up the darkened street to the warehouse. The last time they were all supposed to get together, Miguel had claimed car trouble at the last minute and bailed out on their brunch. But there was no way he was sneaking out of meeting her parents this time—not when they were all on the same piece of property! *I'm halfway there*, Leah thought as they walked through the open front door, *and Miguel doesn't even know it*.

Nicole and Peter greeted them in the entry. "Oh,

Leah!" Peter exclaimed. "Cool costume! You look fantastic."

"Yeah," Nicole echoed gloomily.

Leah was wearing the ornate gold satin dress with the lace shawl draped low on her back. Her hair was curled into a mass of tight brown ringlets, held away from her face with combs, and the rest of her costume was makeup. A thick, pale pancake foundation gave her a skin a sickly, almost bluish pallor. Her lipstick was dark red. And on her neck were two incredibly real-looking puncture wounds, spaced exactly as if made by fangs, complete with rivulets of bright fake blood trickling down to her exposed collarbone.

"Thanks," said Leah, pleased. "I thought that with Jesse being a vampire I might as well dress up like—"

"He bit you," Nicole finished for her. "I wish I'd thought of that."

Nicole was dressed like a cross between Morticia and Elvira, in a tight, low-cut black dress with a long black-and-gray-striped wig. Peter was simply dressed all in black.

"What's up with your costume?" Leah asked him. "I thought you were haunting the graveyard."

"I've got a ghost thing to put on over this, don't worry. I'm just waiting until all the chaperones get here." He glanced expectantly toward Leah's parents.

162

I haven't introduced them yet, Leah suddenly realized. She did so quickly, wondering where Miguel was.

"It's nice to know you," Peter told her parents politely. "All the chaperones are working outside tonight, except for Chris and a couple of his friends. My parents have set up headquarters on the side of the building, with hot coffee and chairs if you need to rest. Can I take you out to meet them?"

The next minute, he was herding them off to join the other adults. Leah knew they'd all be keeping an eye on the line, selling tickets, making sure no one snuck in the backdoor, and patrolling the perimeter of the building. They were also equipped with a first-aid kit and Melanie's cellular phone, in the unlikely event that someone got hurt. It seemed Eight Prime had thought of everything.

"Where's Miguel?" Leah asked Nicole eagerly. "I want to see his costume before we open."

"You'd better hurry, then," Nicole told her. "People are already starting to line up."

Leah turned around, startled. Nicole was right. It was still half an hour before the opening, but an adult Leah didn't recognize was directing several people to the place on the pavement where the line would start.

"I will," Leah promised, taking off through the haunted house.

She found Miguel in the crypt, fussing with the lights. "Hi!" she said breathlessly. "What are you doing?"

"Trying to get this light to shine on the coffin." He stepped down off an overturned crate. "Why, you look downright edible," he teased when he saw her vampire-victim costume.

Leah laughed. "And you're enough to make a girl lose her appetite."

Since Miguel's job was to lie in the coffin, he was dressed like a body someone had dug up. His pants and shirt were shredded to look decayed, and a mixture of brown and gray makeup covered his skin in streaks. His hair was full of dirt and leaves, and one side of his face wore a mask that looked like flesh falling away from the bone. The effect was grim in the extreme, and the plastic worms and leeches hanging from his jaw and bare forearms only added to the revulsion factor.

"You're going to scare the kids to death," Leah said.

"Do you think so?" he asked hopefully.

"You're scaring me."

"I'll show you scary," Miguel promised, grabbing for her waist with a mischievous gleam in his eyes.

"Miguel!" she squealed, skipping out of reach. "You're going to mess up our makeup."

"*Our* makeup? I never thought I'd hear that

excuse," he grumbled, returning to his lighting project.

"What's wrong with the lights?" Leah asked. "They look all right to me."

"No, they're all messed up. I want this one to shine over there," Miguel said, pointing off to a corner. "And this one down on me. It'll be scarier that way."

"Well, can't it wait a minute? There's someone I want you to meet."

Miguel looked down from his crate with a slightly wary expression. "Who?"

"My parents!" she said, pleased with her surprise. "They're dying to meet you."

Her announcement didn't have exactly the effect she had hoped for. "Now?" he demanded. "Here? I can't meet them now."

"Why not?"

"I'm busy, for one thing."

"There's nothing wrong with those lights," Leah said a little impatiently.

"They're not right, Leah. I have to fix them."

"Fix them in a minute, then. It's not like we're going to be outside talking all night."

"I told you, I don't have time. Besides, I'd rather not meet your parents for the first time when I'm dressed like a half-decayed corpse."

"They don't care, Miguel. For Pete's sake—"

"*I* care, Leah. It's embarrassing."

"But it doesn't matter!"

"I'm not having this conversation anymore," he said, turning his back on her and fiddling with the lighting. "I'm too busy, and even if I wasn't, I don't want people in line to see me before they come in."

"You don't *want* to meet them!" Leah accused angrily. "Why don't you be a man and admit it instead of blaming it on the stupid lights?"

"I don't want to meet them *now*," he corrected, wheeling around. "And I already said that, so what's to admit? What's your problem tonight, anyway?"

"My problem is you!" she almost shouted. "I'm sick of your secrets and childish behavior! I've never known anyone who could make a bigger deal out of something so insignificant."

"You're right—it *is* insignificant. So why don't you drop it, for once? Believe it or not, the world will keep turning if we don't meet each other's parents. You're obsessed with this, Leah, I swear."

The last remnants of self-control deserted her. She was so angry she barely knew what she was saying. "I'm obsessed?" she flung back. "I must have been *possessed* to ever go out with you."

"Knock it off, Leah." Miguel's voice was low and strained, as if he feared they'd be overheard.

"Oh, I'll knock it off, all right," she said, more loudly than ever. "I'll knock it off when you march your butt outside and say hello to my parents."

"I'm not going to do it, so drop it."

Leah stared at him in disbelief. The tightly laced bodice of her dress was suddenly impossible to breathe in as her chest heaved upward for air. She took a small step forward, her entire body trembling.

"You know what, Miguel? I *will* drop it. And I'm dropping you, too. I never want to see you again!"

"Aw, come on, Leah. You don't mean that."

He started to climb off his crate, to stretch out a hand . . .

She stared at him one last time, then turned and ran from the room.

I can't believe she did that, Miguel thought again, lying motionless in his coffin.

The haunted house had been open for over an hour and they were getting a great turnout—tons of CCHS students, even more junior high kids, and most of the Junior Explorers with their parents—but Miguel was still too angry at Leah to take any pleasure in Eight Prime's success.

Who does she think she is?

She had always been unreasonable about having their parents in on their relationship, but tonight had been the last straw. How dare she spring something like that on him at the last minute, without any kind of warning?

There was a scuffling at the door to the crypt.

Miguel took a deep breath and held it, then closed his eyes, relying on his ears to give him his cue.

"Ooh, gross, a coffin!" a girl's voice squealed.

"And there's somebody inside it!" whispered another.

Miguel could hear the steps coming nearer. To help maintain an element of surprise, people were being sent through the haunted house in groups spaced a couple of minutes apart. This group sounded big.

"That's just a dummy," an older boy scoffed. "Like the dummy in the other room, remember?"

"It looks real," a fourth voice insisted.

A finger brushed Miguel's shirt, then tentatively prodded his chest.

"Rrrauughhhh!" Miguel howled, sitting bolt upright.

The girls in the group nearly screamed themselves silly, and the boys lost no time running out behind them. Miguel lay down again to wait for the next group, and his mind returned to Leah.

I don't know why she couldn't understand that I was busy with the lights. It was almost like she picked that fight on purpose. And her attitude! Bossing me around like we're married or something!

Even if he'd had time for such stupid games, it wasn't as if he didn't have a few other things on his mind.

I'm glad that I didn't tell her about Mom's kidney disease, he thought. He'd been planning to, especially since he'd already spilled the beans to Peter, but she hadn't exactly given him a chance. *She'd just have made a big scene about that, too. Ever since she won that stupid modeling contest, she hasn't been the same.* He scowled. *She's getting a big head, that's the problem.*

He thought again of the abrupt, senseless way she had just broken up with him and his anger rekindled so hotly that he could barely keep from punching the boards of his coffin. Then he heard more footsteps approaching and he took several deep breaths, trying to calm down enough to hold perfectly still. The footsteps drew nearer, accompanied by giggles and whispers.

Well, that's fine with me, Miguel thought. *If Leah wants to break up, I don't care one bit. It's not like I can't get another girlfriend tomorrow.*

The footsteps were right beside him. Miguel jumped up from his coffin with such a savage howl that the kids he'd just taken by surprise screamed hysterically, turning and running back the way they'd come instead of forward, toward the exit.

"No, wait!" he hollered after them.

An enormous scream a few rooms away let him know that his group had just collided with the next one coming through in the opposite direction.

"Great," he grumbled, climbing out of his coffin. Now he'd have to go gather everyone up and convince them to run toward the exit.

Wait, he thought suddenly. *What if they all met up in Leah's room?*

The possibility stopped him where he stood. He wasn't going in there. No way. Little Miss High-and-Mighty could handle the situation without him.

Miguel walked slowly back to his coffin. Then, with an angry kick at the crates that supported it, he kept going—past his station, past the partition walls, and into the dark, undecorated warehouse beyond. He knew he'd have to return in a moment, but he'd wait until Leah got everyone turned around and safely through his crypt.

The last thing he wanted was to run into her.

In fact, he didn't care if he never saw her again.

Thirteen

After school on Friday, Jesse walked slowly through the silent gymnasium to keep an appointment with Coach Davis. The Wildcats weren't practicing because Clearwater Crossing wasn't playing that night, and it seemed as if everyone else had gone home early too. His footsteps echoed hollowly as he made his way to the coach's office.

"Jones, nice of you to drop in!" the coach boomed sarcastically. Jesse checked his watch—he was barely a minute late.

"Uh, yeah," he said nervously.

The coach waved him to a seat, then leaned back in his own chair on the other side of the desk. "So how are you doing?" he asked.

Jesse wasn't sure how to answer. "All right, I guess. I mean, you know."

Coach Davis shook his head. "I *don't* know. That's why I'm asking."

"Well, how do you expect me to be?" Jesse countered, letting his guard slip a little. "I'm off the team. People all over school are talking about me,

171

but hardly anyone's talking to me. This has got to be the biggest screwup of my life. Coach, please let me play again. The homecoming game is next week and if—"

"You're off for homecoming," Coach Davis broke in. "I already said that, and that's a definite."

"But if—"

"Jones, be quiet!"

Jesse shut his mouth.

"I'm not going to argue with you," said the coach in a slightly calmer voice. "You see, I hold all the cards."

"Yes, sir." Jesse looked at the floor.

"I take it, though, that you're still motivated to rejoin the team?"

"It's all I think about," Jesse answered earnestly. "It's practically all I live for. I've learned my lesson, Coach Davis. If you let me play again, you won't be sorry."

The coach tilted back in his chair, as if to think it over. Then he leaned forward and lifted a newspaper clipping off his desk. It was the *Clearwater Herald* article about Eight Prime's haunted house. "I saw you in the paper," he said. "It looks like you've been keeping pretty busy without us."

"Eight Prime doesn't cut into my football time, Coach," Jesse said immediately. "I've been doing that all along, and it's never caused a problem. I'll quit it, though, if you really think it's necessary."

172

"You misunderstand me, Jones," said the coach. "Your stock shot up ten points the morning I read this. I had you pegged for a me-first kind of guy. Working for charity, trying to memorialize Kurt . . . that was about the last thing I expected from you."

"Oh." Jesse hung his head.

"So how's it going with the drinking?"

"Excuse me?"

"The fact of the matter is, I'm thinking of letting you back on the team after homecoming. But—and this is important—only if I'm sure that you're not drinking anymore. And I mean not at all."

Jesse's hopes spiraled upward as the coach spoke of forgiveness, then plummeted again when he heard the condition. Was the coach serious about sticking to that? Could he really be that clueless?

"You have my word," he compromised, "that I'll never drink before a game or on campus again."

"Not good enough," said the coach.

Jesse stifled a groan. What he had just proposed was actually doable. He didn't want to lie to Coach Davis. But if the guy insisted on taking some ridiculously hard-line policy, he was going to be forced into it.

"Look, Coach," he said reasonably. "I know I blew it, and I can understand that you don't want to see me mess up again. But you've got to know that I'm not the only guy on the team who—"

"Are you even aware that it's *illegal* for people your age to drink alcohol?" the coach interrupted.

"Well . . . sure. But—"

"But nothing, Jones. If you want to be a Wildcat again, I'll have your word of honor that you won't touch another drink. Period."

It took all Jesse's self-control to keep his face expressionless. The coach had to be kidding. Either that or he was some sort of extremist. On the other hand, Jesse could hardly afford to make him angry again. Not with so much on the line.

He's probably just saying that because he has to, Jesse reasoned quickly. *I'll bet it's some sort of school policy. He doesn't really care what I do.*

But what if he does? a nervous voice nagged. *What if he really means it?*

A second later, Jesse made up his mind. It didn't matter either way. He'd say anything to get back on the team. Anything it took.

"You have my word, Coach," he said without blinking. "If you let me back on the team, I won't touch another drink."

The coach stared at him so long that Jesse felt as if he were melting in nervous sweat. But he didn't look away. He didn't dare.

"Do you promise?" the coach asked at last.

Sweat trickled down the back of Jesse's neck and soaked the armpits of his shirt. "I promise."

"How long have you been off the team?"

"Two weeks today. But it feels a lot longer."

The coach actually cracked a smile. "I'll bet it does. All right then, Jones, I'll tell you what—if you miss any more practices, you're not going to be any use to me even if I do decide to take you back. So come to practice on Monday. You're still not playing for homecoming, and I'm not promising you'll play after that. But you start practicing again on Monday. And after that, we'll see."

In a daze, Jesse thanked the coach. His legs were half water beneath him as he rose to shake the man's hand. Somehow he made it back through the gym and out to the parking lot. A sharp north wind was blowing, swirling dead leaves around the pavement, but Jesse barely noticed it as he opened his car door and sank into his seat with relief.

He was back on the team.

"Aargh!"

"Ooh, gross!"

"Man, that's sick!"

Leah could tell by the screaming that the most recent group had just run through Miguel's crypt, a couple of rooms away from the ruined-castle room she was haunting as the vampire victim. Because it was Friday night and there was no school the next day, Eight Prime's haunted house was even busier than it had been the night before. A bunch of the

Wildcats had turned out to show they remembered Kurt, and it seemed as if all of Samuel Clemens Junior High was lined up on the pavement outside. Two of Jenna's younger sisters, Maggie and Allison, had plastered their school with fliers.

"Isn't this cool?" Ben demanded, running into Leah's room. "Did you see all the people waiting outside?"

He was dressed as a werewolf—or his and Nicole's version of one, anyway—with a wild brown wig, fangs, and glue-on fur on his face and hands. The effect probably would have been scarier without the horn-rims, but Ben had insisted that he couldn't see without them.

"Yeah. Great," Leah said, unable to muster the slightest enthusiasm. She knew she ought to be happy, but all she could think about was Miguel.

"What are you doing here?" she added. "I thought you were working with Peter in the graveyard."

"Chris is back there now and he's giving everybody heart attacks," Ben reported proudly.

Leah had seen Chris earlier. He was wearing plain black clothes and the secondhand white hockey mask Nicole had bought. It made an amazingly effective costume, and Leah could imagine how the effect would multiply when Chris leapt out from behind an oversized tombstone.

"So then, what are Courtney and Jeff doing?"

"Courtney's helping Nicole, and Jeff's chained

himself to a wall back there. He's acting like we caught him going through and now we're torturing him or something." Ben shuddered. "Creepy."

There was a sound of approaching footsteps.

"Hide somewhere," Leah whispered to Ben. He crouched in a dark corner, and Leah stood to one side of the room, letting her head loll back and her eyes glaze over. She'd discovered the night before that simply moaning a little and looking dead on her feet was a better way to scare people with her damsel-beyond-distress bit than trying to surprise them. There was a burst of giggling, then a rush of footsteps as a group of girls entered the room.

Leah groaned and swayed slightly.

"Yuck," someone said. "Look at her."

They huddled up a little tighter.

"Is she real?" someone else whispered.

"Well, duh."

Leah lurched a little in their direction and everyone backed up.

"Rrrraaahhh!" Ben howled, leaping out of his hiding place behind them. The girls whirled around in a panic to see Ben raking the air with black fingernails, as if to tear them to pieces. One of them actually screamed.

Then he stepped farther out into the light and they started laughing instead.

"A werewolf in glasses? How lame!" a girl scoffed.

Ben stopped raking. "Werewolves can wear glasses," he said defensively.

"Can *not!*" was the giggled reply.

"Can so! What if—what if the person who gets bit and turns *into* a werewolf wears glasses? They're still going to wear them, right? And then, when they become a werewolf, what are they going to do? Take them off with their claws? I don't think so. They might poke out their eye!"

The girls were laughing too hard to debate him.

Leah hurried forward. "Good argument, Ben, but I think we're killing the mood here. You girls need to keep moving, before the next group comes in." She waved them through the room and they went off willingly, laughing all the way.

"I just don't understand it," Ben said sadly when they had gone. "No one's laughing at *Miguel.*"

As if to reinforce his point, hysterical screaming broke out just then from the very same group of girls. "See?"

"I don't know what to tell you, Ben, except maybe find a place where you don't need to see and put your glasses in your pocket. You can't stay here, though," she added. "Our costumes don't make sense together."

"All right. Maybe I can help Melanie." He ran off with a hopeful expression on his furry, bespectacled face.

Leah knew Melanie was wearing a black robe

and an elongated, white skull mask. In the black-and-white room with the strobe light, it was truly frightening when she popped out. Leah wasn't too sure how a werewolf—especially one with all the shock appeal of a hamster—would fit into Melanie's stylized, black-and-white realm, but she'd let Melanie deal with that.

It wasn't as if she didn't have problems enough of her own.

How could I ever have broken up with Miguel? What was I thinking? Her throat tightened and tears filled her eyes as she remembered their fight of the night before. She slipped hurriedly behind a wall of her castle room to compose herself in private.

She had just been so angry when he'd refused to meet her parents that she'd barely known what she was saying. He was so unreasonable, so selfish. That anger had carried her through most of Thursday night. But very late, lying in bed after the haunted house had ended, the full magnitude of what she'd done had finally broken over her and she'd sobbed like a little girl. To never see Miguel again, to never slip her arms around him or kiss the warm brown skin of his neck . . .

A tear rolled down her cheek. Even *thinking* things like that was killing her.

Maybe I could apologize.

But she remembered the way he had looked at her earlier that evening, when Eight Prime had gathered to open the haunted house. His eyes had barely touched her, as if she weren't even there. She doubted he'd accept an apology, even if she could bring herself to try one.

"What have I done?" she moaned.

Never—not for a moment—had she guessed she was going to break up with him.

And now it was already over.

Fourteen

"Is something the matter, *mi hijo?*" Mrs. del Rios asked her son.

"No, nothing," Miguel muttered. "What's taking so long?" He cast an annoyed glance at the receptionist behind the counter, but the woman didn't notice. "They shouldn't make you wait like this. Dialysis takes long enough already."

"Miguel, why don't you go see one of your friends? Do something fun for a change, like Rosa. I can take the bus home."

"No," he said sullenly. If Rosa wanted to run around with her friends, that was her business. For his part, he'd promised to see his mother through every one of her Saturday-morning dialysis appointments, and that was exactly what he'd do.

After all, it wasn't his mother's fault he was in such a rotten mood.

I can't believe Leah broke up with me, he thought miserably. *Not that I didn't deserve it, but still . . . I can't believe I was such a jerk!*

He still couldn't explain, even to himself, why

181

he'd been so afraid to simply say hello to her parents. *Maybe if she hadn't sprung it on me out of nowhere . . .* What if the Rosenthals hadn't liked him? They could have told her to stop seeing him.

Not that it matters now. You took care of that all by yourself.

Miguel glanced at his mother, who waited patiently in the chair next to his. He wished he could tell her what had happened and let her make him feel better. But how could he tell his mom that he and Leah had broken up when she didn't even know they were dating? *I should have told her,* he reproached himself. *Why didn't I?* None of the decisions he had made in the past made any sense to him that morning.

"Mariana?" an unfamiliar nurse called, poking her head into the lobby. "Come with me, please."

Miguel and his mother glanced at each other, surprised, then rose and followed the woman. But instead of leading them to the dialysis equipment, she showed them into a small examination room.

"What's up?" Miguel asked. "Where's Carol? We have a dialysis appointment now."

"Carol's not quite ready for you yet, but Dr. Gibbons wants to speak to your mother," the nurse explained, closing the door as she left.

A few minutes later Dr. Gibbons bustled in, looking slightly harried. "Mariana, good. How are you feeling?" she asked, flipping through a manila folder.

"Fine," Mrs. del Rios answered cautiously. "The same."

"Well, I got your blood work back, so I thought I'd give you the results."

The doctor pulled up a rolling stool and sat down. She was young—too young to be a doctor, Miguel thought—and her frizzy orange hair stuck out like wire in every direction. She closed the chart and leaned forward.

"It's about what we expected," she said, referring to the blood tests she'd sent out earlier that week. "We have a pretty good handle on the anemia now, but your blood pressure . . . I'm going to adjust your medications again. Are you sticking to your diet?"

"Forget the stupid diet!" Miguel broke in before his mother could reply. "You know what she needs is a transplant!"

"Miguel!" Mrs. del Rios said sharply.

"No, that's all right," Dr. Gibbons said, turning to Miguel. "I understand your frustration, Miguel, believe me. Two years is a long time to wait. But there's a growing need for these organs and not enough donors. People are waiting all over the country, some in worse shape than your mother. Try to be patient. Eventually it will be our turn."

"I'm sick of being patient! I've told you and told

you that I'll give her one of mine. How often do I have to say it?" He'd offered so many times before, had been brushed off so many times before.

But this time the doctor finally seemed to hear him.

"I'll keep it in mind," she promised.

"There you are, Caitlin!" Jenna exclaimed, bursting into the garage. "I've been searching for you everywhere!"

Caitlin looked up from brushing the mangy stray dog she'd brought home. "Don't you think her coat looks a lot better?" she asked proudly.

Jenna hesitated. She knew that Caitlin had washed the pitiable mutt—twice—and stuffed it until it couldn't eat another bite, but it was still the scraggliest, most unattractive animal Jenna had ever seen. She could barely believe her mom had given Caitlin permission to keep it in the garage until she could find it a new home. "It, uh, looks a *lot* cleaner," Jenna answered in a flash of inspiration.

At least a person could tell what color it was now: gray—a shaggy, nondescript gray.

"Yes, you're a pretty girl. Aren't you a pretty girl?" Caitlin baby-talked to the dog, actually kissing its black nose. The dog wriggled delightedly and made frantic whining noises. "That's a good girl. What a good girl!" Caitlin cooed.

Jenna watched, so fascinated that she almost forgot why she'd come. She had never seen Cat act so goofy before.

Then she heard Peter's car pull up outside and the purpose of her errand came back in a rush.

"Do you want to help out with the Junior Explorers this morning?" she asked. "The kids are all going to dress up in costume, and Eight Prime is taking them to see the parade. After that a few of the downtown stores are having daytime trick-or-treating, so we'll walk them around for some candy. It ought to be fun."

Caitlin shook her head. "I can't. I have to stay with my dog."

Jenna noticed the unwise use of the word *my*, but decided to overlook it. "So bring the dog with you. It can come, if it's on a leash."

"I don't think that's a good idea," Caitlin said. "She shouldn't be around the kids until a vet looks her over to make sure she's not carrying any diseases."

Jenna's eyes widened. *Oh, but it's okay for you to kiss its snotty nose*, she thought, almost as amazed as disgusted.

"Besides," Caitlin continued, "in a couple of hours, we have an appointment with a vet I found in the phone book. If I went with you I wouldn't be back in time."

Jenna heard the doorbell ring and knew Peter was waiting, but she couldn't tear herself away.

"Mom's taking you and that dog to the vet?" she asked, unable to believe it.

"No." Caitlin looked confused. "Oh, I get it. Because I said *we*, right? I meant me and the dog. Didn't I, baby?" she asked the mutt. "Yes! Oh, that's a good girl." The good girl wagged her scrawny tail ecstatically.

"Jenna!" Maggie yelled from inside the house. "Peter's here!"

"I've got to go," Jenna said hurriedly. "Are you sure you don't want to come?" She'd been hoping to get Caitlin out among people again. "Maura's going to be there."

"No. I can't," Caitlin repeated. She put down the brush and began examining one of the larger sores on the dog's back legs. "Have a good time," she added absently.

"Jenna!" Maggie bellowed at the top of her lungs.

"Okay. See you later." Jenna ran for the door.

It struck her as nothing short of amazing that timid Caitlin was taking a strange dog to a strange vet all by herself. A vet she'd found in the phone book, no less! Now that Jenna was thinking about it, though, Caitlin had always been overprotective of animals, saving baby birds, frogs, squirrels, and anything else that was slow or injured enough to let her catch it. Maybe it was some sort of mothering thing.

Jenna dashed through the den, rounded the corner, and skidded out on the entryway rug.

"Whoa!" Peter laughed as she slid across the hardwood floor, barely jumping off in time to miss colliding with the wall. "Careful!"

"I meant to do that," she told him with perfect dignity.

"Yeah, right. Are you ready?" He was wearing jeans and the white Junior Explorers T-shirt on which she had embroidered his name. The sight of that tired old garment made something tug at her heart, but she wasn't exactly sure why.

"Of course," she said, shaking it off and flashing her brightest smile. "Let's go!"

"Melanie, Melanie let's go there!" Amy begged, tugging on her hand and pointing to the five-and-dime up ahead.

The costume parade down Clearwater Boulevard was over, and Eight Prime was walking the Junior Explorers along the crowded sidewalk for daytime trick-or-treating in a few of the local stores. No one was giving out anything spectacular—a miniature Tootsie Roll here, a lollipop there—but the kids were having a blast just the same. Amy's loot rattled around in the paper sack she'd decorated that morning. She clutched it tightly in the hand that wasn't holding Melanie's.

"I guess we can do that," Melanie replied. She turned to Peter, who was walking along beside her. "Okay?"

"Wherever you guys want to go," he said. Lisa clung to his hand possessively. She was dressed—not surprisingly—as an angel, in a white dress with filmy pink wings and a gold tinsel halo over perfect blond ringlets.

Melanie glanced back down at Amy in her little leopard outfit and smiled. Her costume was of the zip-up footed-pajama variety, made of a beige-colored plush sprinkled liberally with black spots. Amy's face peered eagerly from a hood of the same fabric, complete with matching ears on top. Melanie reached down to tuck a few stray, springy brown curls back inside it.

Through the windows of the five-and-dime, Melanie could see the table set up for the kids right at the front of the store. "Okay, you girls go on in, and Peter and I'll wait here," she told them. The pair hesitated only a second, then took off through the automatic door with a clump of other youngsters.

"They're loving this," Peter remarked, smiling good-naturedly as they disappeared into the crowd. He scanned the sidewalk, looking for the other Junior Explorers, and Melanie followed his gaze. She and Peter had gradually dawdled to the back of the group, and Chris and Maura were at the front, out of sight. In between, the rest of Eight Prime was working at keeping an eye on sixteen excited Junior Explorers.

Melanie saw Miguel up ahead, watching the kids from the edge of the sidewalk. He was scowling as if not enjoying the crowded scene in front of him.

Where's Leah? Melanie wondered. She finally spotted her way up ahead, holding hands with Priscilla and Elton. Melanie's eyes narrowed reflectively.

Leah and Miguel were never obvious about hanging out together, but ever since Melanie had inadvertently learned they were a couple, she'd noticed they weren't often apart. For the last couple of days, though, she hadn't seen them together once—not even to say hello.

"I wonder if those two had a fight," she mused out loud.

"Who?" Peter asked.

"Leah and Miguel," she answered without thinking. "They're acting like they broke up or something."

Too late, she slapped a restraining hand over her mouth. "Oh, no," she groaned, squeezing her eyes shut. "You didn't just hear me say that, Peter. Please, I promised I wouldn't tell *anyone*. I can't believe I have such a big mouth!"

Peter shrugged. "Don't worry. You didn't tell me anything new. I've been wondering the same thing, actually."

"You knew about them?" Melanie asked, stunned. "How did you know?"

"I'd rather not say." A strange look appeared in his eyes. "But Jenna knows too."

"And do they know you know?"

"Not a clue," Peter said, a smile edging onto his lips.

It *was* kind of funny. The way things were going, everyone in the group would know before those two actually got around to telling anyone. Assuming there was anything still to tell . . .

"How did Jenna find out?"

Peter looked up the sidewalk to where his best friend and Nicole were shepherding more kids. The expression in his eyes had deepened from strange to completely unreadable. "I can't really answer that."

"All right," Melanie said quickly, not wanting to put him on the spot.

She couldn't be sure, but she was starting to get the impression that something wasn't quite right between Peter and Jenna either.

Fifteen

Nicole pulled on her long black wig as the door-bell rang again. It wasn't completely dark yet, but the trick-or-treaters were already showing up. She could hear the low rumble of her father's voice downstairs as he greeted the kids and passed out candy, and she nervously stepped up her prepara-tions for the last night of the haunted house.

It's incredible that it's already almost over, she thought as she drew around her bright blue eyes with a thick black lining pencil. It seemed just the other day that Ben had first suggested it and they'd almost written it off as too complicated. What a lot had happened since then! They'd had a good turnout on Thursday night, and an even better one on Friday. They'd already taken in nearly three thousand dollars. And even though Nicole was miss-ing the big Halloween party that night, she didn't mind anymore. What they were doing was just as fun.

Besides, everyone was bringing cookies or candy or something special that night to celebrate

Halloween, and Nicole couldn't wait until they got a look at her witch's brew—a green punch over a lump of dry ice that made fog boil up to the surface then float dramatically down to the floor. It was sure to make an impression, and she smiled to imagine her friends' reactions.

Although Courtney's bound to be hating life, she thought, pausing with the pencil. Jeff was really into the haunted house. The tourist-in-chains bit he'd come up with the night before was great, and people had started moving a whole lot faster through that lonely section of warehouse. Courtney, on the other hand, had been forcing a smile that looked like a facial tic for the last two nights, barely managing to maintain the appearance of being there voluntarily as she drifted from station to station. Tonight, with the missed party to add to her list of grievances, she was likely to be in an even worse mood than before.

Oh well. If she is, I'll just hang out with Leah. Nicole reached for the black lipstick and started putting it on. Of course, Leah hadn't exactly been a party animal the last two evenings, either. Something was eating her . . . and Nicole was pretty sure it was the U.S. Girls contest. She wasn't *saying* she was going to drop out every two minutes anymore, but Nicole could almost feel her thinking it. She'd never met anyone less appreciative of her own good luck.

At least Jesse's in a good mood, she thought, smiling with freshly blackened lips. He'd been on top of the world since his meeting with Coach Davis the afternoon before. Friday night he'd been the most fearsome creature in the haunted house. And that morning, at the Halloween parade, Nicole was pretty sure he'd been flirting with her. Well, maybe not *flirting*. But teasing. Paying attention, anyway. Considering all the pressure he'd been under, she'd decided to forgive him for telling her to shut up.

And the best part was that he still wasn't talking to Melanie.

I wonder if he's going to the homecoming dance, Nicole thought. He was sitting out the homecoming game, but it seemed certain he'd be back on the team after that. He could hold his head up around school again, so there was no reason *not* to go to the dance.

Who will he take? she dared to wonder. *If only he'd ask me!*

He *had* been paying a lot more attention to her since he'd had that fight with Melanie. As far as she knew, he hadn't asked anyone else. . . .

Maybe I ought to start shopping for a dress, just in case, she thought hopefully, picking up a bruise-colored blush. *Something slinky, to show off my hipbones.*

She dropped her free hand to feel them jutting

through the fabric of her dress. Ever since that horrible night she'd made herself vomit, Nicole had been back on her diet with a vengeance.

She smiled at the reassuring hardness of bone beneath her fingers.

If Jesse didn't ask her to the dance, maybe she'd even ask him.

Miguel slipped out the back door of the warehouse and into the cold night air. He'd been cramped in that coffin for the last two hours, his throat was sore from three nights of shouting, and he really needed a break. He drifted across a short stretch of pavement and lost himself in the shadow of trees at the edge of the lot.

It was getting late, and things should have been winding down, but there was still an amazingly long line for the haunted house. Most of the patrons so far that night had been parents with younger kids, but Miguel did see a couple of people he recognized from CCHS, despite the party going on. Then, near the end of the line, he spotted Kurt Englbehrt's old girlfriend, Dana Fraser. She seemed to be alone, and Miguel hesitated only a second before he struck out across the lot.

"Dana! Hi," he said, reaching her side.

She turned and smiled vacantly, as if not really sure who he was. He had forgotten about his costume and makeup.

"Oops, sorry. Miguel del Rios, remember?" he prompted.

"Sure," she said, nodding vaguely. Her eyes met his a moment, then wandered aimlessly off.

She didn't look good. Miguel didn't want to be critical, but he was surprised by her appearance. From a distance, Dana's shining blond hair had looked the same, but up close her skin was pale, and he could see that she'd lost a lot of weight. Too much weight. Under her eyes, dark circles sank into sallow cheeks, and her eyes themselves were glassy and far away. Miguel could barely believe that the person in front of him now was the pretty, spirited girl Kurt had been so in love with.

"You don't have to stand in line," he told her, tugging at her sleeve. "Come on up to the front. You can be our guest."

"Huh?" she said, trying to focus her glassy eyes.

"I said come to the front," he repeated. "You can go through for free."

She seemed to think a minute. "No, I want to wait. And I definitely want to pay. That's why I'm here. To help y'all get Kurt's bus."

"But, well . . ."

He didn't know what to say to her. He wasn't sure she was listening anyway. It was spooky, really, how much she had changed.

"Don't you at least want to say hello to everyone else? I know they would really like to see you."

195

She nodded. They stood looking at each other a minute.

"What?" she asked.

"Nothing," he said, disconcerted. "Are you sure you won't cut the line?"

"No. I'm fine." She didn't look fine.

"All right, then," he said uneasily. "See you later."

Dana didn't answer. It was as if in her mind he had already gone.

She's not dealing with Kurt's death at all, Miguel thought as he walked back toward the warehouse. She'd seemed so lost in space, in fact, that Miguel wasn't sure the damage he'd seen was due to grief alone. He could imagine what she was going through, though. He could imagine it too well.

I don't know how I'd cope if Leah died, he thought, sneaking in through the backdoor. *That would be so awful.* Even the thought made him sick.

And suddenly he knew what he had to do.

Weaving quickly through the haunted house, he reached his crypt room and kept going, not even pausing to scare kids coming through from the other direction. Another few seconds and he was in Leah's castle.

"Leah!" he called loudly.

She turned, startled. Her hazel eyes were wide with surprise, and her long hands twisted the lace of her shawl. Even in pancake makeup and that disgusting shade of lipstick, she was so beautiful she nearly took his breath away.

"Leah, I'm sorry," he said without pausing. "I was an idiot—a total jerk. I don't know what got into me."

"But why—" she began.

"I don't know why! I only know I can't lose you. Not like this." He took a step forward and reached for her hands. "I—I love you, Leah. Can you forgive me?"

She stared at him a moment, then burst into happy tears. "I love you, too," she sobbed, throwing herself into his arms. "Oh, Miguel, I missed you so much. You have no idea."

"I think I have *some* idea," he whispered, a catch in his voice. He had never seen her cry before, and the experience made his own feelings that much stronger. It was a miracle just to have her in his arms.

"Let's never fight again," Leah said, raising her tear-streaked face. "I can't stand it."

"No, me either. I'm sorry I started that one. I've just been so on edge lately. My . . . my mom's kind of sick. That doesn't excuse my being such a jerk, though," he added quickly.

Leah sniffed and wiped at her eyes. "What's wrong with your mom?"

"It's her kidneys. I worry about her sometimes, and I guess it got to me."

"Is it serious?" she asked, concerned.

"Well . . ." He was reluctant to go into details just then, especially when there was still a chance Leah would be mad at him for not telling her before. "They can fix it. She'll be fine."

Leah hesitated, then hugged him again, her face buried into his neck. "I'm glad," she murmured, taking a deep breath.

Just then a loud scream in the next room let them know another group was coming. Leah tensed up and Miguel dropped his arms in their old, instinctive pattern of not letting anyone see them touching.

But then Leah reached out and took his hand. "If we're going to be together, I can't do this anymore," she said. "I'm tired of sneaking around, pretending I barely know you. If I'm going to be your girlfriend, I want everyone to know it."

He wanted that too, he realized. "You mean Eight Prime and *everyone*?" he asked, just to make sure.

"Everyone," she repeated.

He smiled. "Might as well start now, then." He bent to kiss her just as a rowdy, screaming group of junior-high kids ran into the room.

"Ooh, sick!" one of the guys yelled. "That chick's letting a dead guy kiss her!"

"Unh-uh," a girl told him scornfully. "He's biting her. Look at her neck."

"That's from a vampire, stupid. That dude's not a vampire."

"Then why is he biting her?"

There was more discussion along those lines, but Miguel barely heard it as he pulled Leah tightly to his body, his mouth soft and warm against hers. When he finally let her go, the kids were several rooms away and completely forgotten.

"There. Is that out in the open enough for you?" he teased, wanting to kiss her that way all night. "Should we go do that in front of Eight Prime?"

"Yeah, sure," Leah replied playfully. "Promises, promises."

"You don't believe me?" He grabbed her hand, prepared to drag her out and kiss her in every room of the haunted house. "I'll do it."

He would have, too, but Leah shook her head. "Everyone's working now. Let's tell them after we close."

"Well . . . okay."

"And Miguel? When I said that I wanted to tell *everyone* about us, I meant our parents, too. I want you to visit my house, and I want to be welcome at yours. I want to call you whenever I feel like it. I want everything in the open from this day forward."

"Right. I kind of figured that." The whole idea still made him nervous, but it wasn't as if he could argue. They'd just gotten back together—the last thing he needed was another fight.

Stop worrying, he told himself. *It'll be fine*.

"Everyone is going to know," he assured her. "I'll get one of those biplanes to drag a banner over school if it'll make you feel better."

Leah smiled. "Promise?"

"Promise."

Sixteen

"Come on," Leah said, taking Miguel's hand and leading him up to the lobby of the haunted house.

They exchanged brief, bittersweet smiles, as if acknowledging the end of something great—their secret relationship—but at the same time looking forward to the start of something better—their official one. Then the last few yards passed under their feet and they joined the rest of Eight Prime. Everyone was standing around the card table and cash box, except Nicole, who was seated on a crate, counting money.

"Miguel and I have something to say," Leah announced.

Six heads swiveled their way. Then everyone seemed to notice her hand clasped in Miguel's, and all eyes flew to their faces.

"We're together," Miguel said simply.

Nicole jumped up from her crate. "Congratulations!" she cried. "Oh, you guys, that's so great! You look so cute together."

"Real cute," Leah laughed, gesturing toward their costumes.

"Oh, but you will. You know what I mean. Wow, I'm so happy for you!"

"Yes, congratulations," Melanie chimed in, apparently deciding to play it dumb.

Everyone else was smiling and nodding, but Leah couldn't help noticing that Nicole was the only one who looked surprised. Jenna, Peter, Jesse, and even Ben seemed to have already guessed. Apparently she and Miguel weren't quite as clever as they'd thought. Still, it didn't matter anymore . . . and Leah was glad. It felt fantastic to have everything out in the open.

"So how much money did we make?" she asked, dropping Miguel's hand to join the circle around the cash box. He pressed in close beside her.

"I don't know," Nicole admitted. "I kind of forgot where I was."

"Sorry." Leah cast an amused sideways glance at Miguel.

"It's late, anyway," Peter spoke up. "Everyone's tired. Why don't we meet here to clean up tomorrow, and we can work out our finances then? We'll figure out how much we made over all three days."

"Good idea," Jenna said quickly. "Because I really have to go."

"Fine with me," echoed Ben. "I have to leave now too."

They agreed to meet at two o'clock the following afternoon, and minutes later the group broke up.

Leah walked through the dimly lit parking lot hand in hand with Miguel, finally set free from so many secrets. Everything was out in the open now. Soon their parents would know, and so would everyone at school. Everything was honest, all aboveboard. It was the most liberating feeling—Leah wanted to fly.

Then a nasty, unwelcome voice piped up in her head. *Not everything is out in the open*, it said. *There's still the fact that you spied on him.*

Leah grimaced. How she wished she'd never done that! For a moment she even considered telling him. They were almost to his car—if she hurried she could blurt it out quick, before they got in.

But what if he got mad? Was it really worth risking just to ease her guilty conscience?

No, she decided as Miguel opened her car door. *That's one little secret I'll just have to keep.*

Jenna ripped off her costume in the back of the warehouse, struggling to keep from crying. No matter how hard she tried to be reasonable, Miguel and Leah's announcement still struck her as nothing short of cruel.

And that wasn't even the worst of it. Peter had been hanging out with Melanie ever since that morning.

First during the parade, then trick-or-treating with the Junior Explorers, they'd stuck together like magnets. Jenna had been so excited about having him drive her to the park, but it had turned out to be a formality. He'd barely even noticed her once they'd arrived. Then, on the drive home, he'd told her he was giving *Melanie* a ride to the haunted house that night . . . oh, and could Jenna get there on her own?

"Probably," she'd said. "But why can't the three of us ride together?"

"Well, we *could*," Peter had admitted. "But Melanie's bringing cupcakes, and my mom made all those cookies. And we've got our costumes and everything too. I thought it would just be easier . . . if you don't mind, I mean."

"I *hate* this!" Jenna said now as she forced pieces of her costume into a too-small canvas tote bag. Of course she minded! Wasn't it bad enough that she'd already lost the only guy she'd ever liked to Leah? Did she have to lose her best friend to Melanie too?

"What are you doing back here?" Peter asked, stepping around her partition. "It's practically pitch black."

"I'm putting away my costume," Jenna told him angrily. "Is that all right with you?" She stuffed the last piece into her bag and jumped up to face him, glaring.

"Okay, okay. Don't bite my head off. I just

wanted to make sure you were okay with . . ." He hesitated. "I'm ready to lock up."

Apparently he'd decided not to mention Leah and Miguel. It was the right move, but Jenna was still furious.

"Go right ahead," she said sarcastically, pushing by him and heading for the door. "I wouldn't want to inconvenience you and *Melanie.*"

"Jenna, wait," he called after her. "What's the matter? You're not mad at me, are you?"

"At you? Oh, no," she sneered in a voice that said just the opposite. "Why would I be mad at *you?*"

She pushed the front door of the warehouse open and began to run. She had parked her mother's station wagon down the street, just a block or so away. All she wanted was to reach its shelter, to finally let loose the tears that clogged her throat and burned at her eyelids.

"Jenna! Would you wait a minute?" Peter yelled from the doorway, but she kept running.

She'd parked farther down the street than she'd remembered, and it was dark away from the parking-lot lights. Wind sighed through the half-naked trees, but every other sound ceased as she hurried past the overgrown property bordering the road. No frogs, no crickets, no birds . . . The tangled bushes at the roadside crouched dead silent in the darkness.

Anything could be hiding in there, she thought. *Anything*. The idea was frightening enough to take the edge off her anger as she hurried the last few yards, fumbling with her keys.

And then a sound in the darkness behind her almost stopped her heart. It was footsteps. They darted out from the bushes . . . they were coming right at her. Jenna whirled to face her attacker, her heart in her throat.

"Hi, Jenna!" cried a docile-looking werewolf. It was Ben.

He must have been waiting here for me to come to my car, she realized. She was so relieved, she almost felt nauseous.

"Hi, Ben," she said, her heart still hammering. "What's the matter? Need a ride?"

"No. My dad's coming pretty soon." He stood shuffling his feet, looking at her expectantly.

"Well, uh, that's good." She unlocked the driver's door and tossed her tote bag into the backseat.

Ben was still standing there.

"Is he picking you up here?" she asked, at a loss.

"Yeah. Pretty soon."

"Okay, then. I guess I'll see you tomorrow." She started to climb into her seat.

"Jenna, wait!" Ben rushed around the car, hurriedly grabbing her door to keep her from closing it.

"What?"

"I was, uh, wondering," he said awkwardly. "I

mean . . . if you're not . . . Would you want to go to the homecoming dance with me?"

Melanie watched, torn, as Peter withdrew the key and rattled the warehouse door to make sure he'd locked it securely. There was something bothering him, and she was pretty sure she knew what.

"I saw Jenna go running out of here," she said. "Do you want to talk about it?"

He shrugged as they headed for his car. He had parked behind the warehouse that night. "We had a little fight, I guess. I'm not exactly sure."

"You're not sure if you had a fight?" Melanie asked, surprised.

"Well, I'm pretty sure we had a fight. I just don't know what it was about."

They reached his Toyota and he let them in. They buckled their seat belts. But Peter didn't start the car. Instead he sat staring into space, a bewildered expression in his blue eyes.

"I hope *I* didn't have anything to do with it," Melanie said finally. "She wasn't upset because you were driving me tonight, was she?"

"No. I don't see why she would be. There's just . . . there're some things going on, and . . . I don't know."

He obviously wasn't telling her everything. Melanie decided her guess had been right after all.

"Well, maybe you and I ought to steer clear of each other awhile anyway," she said reluctantly. "I mean, you and Jenna are best friends, and she may not like me taking up so much of your time. If I was Jenna, I'd probably be jealous." It nearly killed her to say so, because she didn't want to steer clear of Peter. But she didn't want to make trouble between him and Jenna, either.

"No. Avoiding each other would be pointless. It's just . . . well, I can't explain it. But Jenna isn't jealous of *you*—we aren't that way. And there's nothing romantic between us either, if that's what you're thinking. Jenna just had a bad night."

Melanie was surprised by how relieved she was to hear that. Especially the part about there being nothing romantic . . .

Peter was reaching to turn the car key in the ignition. Overcome by a sudden impulse, Melanie reached out and put her hand over his, stopping him. He turned to look at her, his expression puzzled.

She leaned toward him. Their eyes locked.

Slowly, uncertainly, she brought her mouth to his and kissed him on the lips.

Seventeen

Miguel tossed restlessly in his single bed, unable to sleep. It was late—hours past midnight—but he was more awake now than when he'd first lain down. He'd never fall asleep at this rate.

He just couldn't stop thinking of Leah. He was relieved to have made up with her earlier that night. It was such a big weight off his heart. Yet he couldn't help worrying about all the pitfalls he saw in their future.

Worse, he couldn't stop worrying about his mother.

He was sure Dr. Gibbons had been trying to tell them something that morning, trying to prepare them for something. . . .

He sat up abruptly, too restless to keep still. He had to get out, had to do something. Slipping out of the blankets, he pulled on the jeans he'd discarded on the floor, forced his sockless feet into shoes, and zipped his old bomber jacket—the one that had been his father's—over his bare skin.

It was cold outside when he opened the door.

The night was moonless but crystal clear, and a million tiny stars shone sharply overhead. Miguel eased silently through the doorway and locked the house behind him.

His shoes squished in the grass as he walked out to the street, and he felt the cold seeping up through their soles. His breath made crystalline puffs out in front of him. Pushing his hands more deeply into his pockets, he reached the pavement, turned, and began walking along the side of the road. There was no traffic in the neighborhood at that hour. Everything was still. Miguel's own breathing and the soft tattoo of his sneakers on asphalt were the only sounds he heard.

He didn't know where he was going. He wasn't going anywhere in particular. He cruised the silent streets simply for the release of moving his arms and legs, of taking in cold air and breathing out warm. The entire town was asleep, but he was awake, alert . . . alive.

And then he turned a corner and stopped. The spires of his old church were outlined against the starry sky, defiantly piercing the night. The sight was incredibly beautiful, and however he felt about church, there was no denying the power of that sharp silhouette. Instead of turning away, as he had so many times before, Miguel drew nearer, something tugging at his memory.

It's All Saints Day, he recalled. *November first.*

There would be a special mass that morning. Miguel continued his walk toward the church, remembering other All Saints Days, when he'd been an altar boy and his whole family had watched proudly from a pew. Kurt Englbehrt had been an altar boy too then. Now Kurt was dead . . . and Mr. del Rios was dead . . .

Miguel felt something icy slide down his cheek and realized he was crying. He kept walking, onto the grounds of the church, hurrying blindly down the side of the silent stone building to a door he knew was never locked. He reached it, rested his hand on the cold metal handle, then slowly pushed it open.

The church was dark inside except for a low light over the altar and a bank of candles to one side. The sight of it, the familiar smell, washed over him, sparking memories he thought he'd buried for good. In his mind he saw his father's casket again, up at the front of the aisle, and Father Sebastian sprinkling it with holy water, fogging it with incense. He saw his mother and sister crying in the front pew and the fourteen-year-old he'd once been, stone-faced beside them, determined to show no weakness to a god who could let all that happen.

But he saw other things as well. Himself in his altar boy robes, half proud, half awed as he assisted at the mass. The old women of the church, kneeling to take communion as if it were more to them than the air they breathed. His sister, Rosa, in the blue robes of the Virgin Mary, holding center stage in a long-ago Christmas pageant.

He walked farther inside with faltering steps, his eyes fixed on the altar. At the first pew he dipped a knee and crossed himself. Then he froze. He hadn't intended to do that.

Old habits die hard, he thought bitterly, betrayed by his own actions. And then his tears came in earnest. They weren't just habits once. The genuflecting, the crossing . . . those things had meant something important. Overcome, Miguel dropped to his knees, the anger and grief of the last three years bursting through the walls he'd built around them in a prayer that was almost a howl.

God, if you're listening, if you ever did listen to me, why did you make me hate you? Why did you do this to us? Weren't we good enough? Didn't we try to be good? So then why did you take my father? How come you had to pick him?

And what about Mom and her kidney disease? What about public assistance? Is it some type of joke with you to see how much we can take? Well, you win, all right? We can't take very much more.

Sobs racked his body, and his knuckles turned white on the back of the pew he gripped. *Please, God. No more. Let my mother get well. Let my father be with you. And me . . . let me not be so sad and afraid anymore. Please, God . . .*

There was more as Miguel prayed for his family, for himself, and for an end to the anguish of the last three years. When he had finished, he opened his eyes and rose shakily to his feet, disoriented by emotion.

The glow of candles caught his attention first, each one lit in hopes of an answered prayer. He stumbled toward them; their separate flames blurred through his tears into a single, larger fire. Shoving his hand deep in his pocket, Miguel removed a crumpled dollar bill and bought a candle from the box. He set it into position with the others, then struck the long match and lit it with a shaking hand.

Dear God, he prayed. *If you make my mother well, I promise I'll never doubt you again.*

Find out what happens next in Clearwater Crossing #5, *Just Friends*.

ABOUT THE AUTHOR

Laura Peyton Roberts holds an M.A. in English from San Diego State University. A native Californian, she lives with her husband in San Diego.